With a toss of her head, Katie marched to the front of the room and drew her first dare

She slipped the red velvet ribbon from the crisp parchment, unrolled it and read out loud to the room. "You have drawn a three-part dare. Each of your dares is to be completed within one week's time. The second and third dares will be mailed to you by the Thursday of each week. For this week, your dare is to make love to the man of your fantasies in a forbidden place."

Stunned, Katie turned to gape at the women of the M & B club. It was as if the dare had been tailor-made for her. Correction: tailor-made for the old Katie. The one who used to do foolish things like make love to strangers in closets.

"Ball's in your court, Katie," said Lindsay, the club's president, with a wry smirk on her face. "Are you all talk? Or do you dare?"

Blaze™

Dear Reader,

Welcome to THE MARTINI DARES series. We hope you'll love meeting and getting to know the Winfield sisters and the very sexy men who turn their oh-so-ordered lives upside down.

First up is the youngest sister—impetuous, sexually adventuresome Katie Winfield, who's secretly longing to settle down but doesn't exactly know how to go about it. She's always been the wild child of the family and she wonders exactly who she'll be if she dares to let go of that role.

Enter Liam James, an ambitious, hardworking real estate mogul on the verge of making his first cool billion. He's in need of a good time as badly as Katie needs emotional security. But he's not about to admit it, even though he's wildly attracted to the high-society graphic artist he's just hired to run his new advertising campaign.

Then Katie joins the mysterious Martinis & Bikinis, a club formed to help empower women in their sexual lives by issuing them provocative dares. All bets are off as Katie performs one sexy Martini Dare after another on an unsuspecting Liam, loosening him and reforming his workaholic ways.

But can a very bad girl find happiness with a very good man?

Don't miss the next book in the series, *My Front Page Scandal* by Carrie Alexander. You might just find yourself wanting to do a Martini Dare or two of your very own.

Happy reading!

Lori Wilde

LORI WILDE
My Secret Life

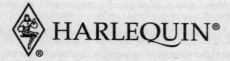

HARLEQUIN®

TORONTO • NEW YORK • LONDON
AMSTERDAM • PARIS • SYDNEY • HAMBURG
STOCKHOLM • ATHENS • TOKYO • MILAN • MADRID
PRAGUE • WARSAW • BUDAPEST • AUCKLAND

ISBN-13: 978-0-373-79350-1
ISBN-10:   0-373-79350-2

MY SECRET LIFE

ABOUT THE AUTHOR

Lori Wilde is the author of thirty-nine books. She's been nominated for a RITA® Award and four *Romantic Times BOOKreviews* Reviewers' Choice Awards. Her books have been excerpted in *Cosmopolitan*, *Redbook* and *Quick & Simple*. Lori teaches writing online through Ed2go. She's an R.N. trained in forensics, and volunteers at a battered women's shelter.

Books by Lori Wilde

HARLEQUIN BLAZE

Don't miss any of our special offers. Write to us at the following address for information on our newest releases.

Harlequin Reader Service
U.S.: 3010 Walden Ave., P.O. Box 1325, Buffalo, NY 14269
Canadian: P.O. Box 609, Fort Erie, Ont. L2A 5X3

For April Birchell

Thanks so much for the inside scoop on graphic artists and for sharing your own secret life story with me. You're living proof that daring to follow your heart is worth the risk.

1

KATIE WINFIELD plotted the seduction with military precision.

Exactitude wasn't her typical modus operandi. On the contrary, she was usually quite spontaneous and, in fact, had a reputation as something of a free spirit. But she and Richard had been flirting for weeks with no forward motion in their relationship. Tonight would thrust them toward a whole new level of intimacy.

Embracing the advance planning she normally eschewed, Katie picked up a pencil and ticked off the items on her To Do list.

Facial and pedicure. Check.

Sexy French-maid costume. Check.

Tantalizing new perfume. Check.

Catch-me, do-me stilettos. Check.

Auburn wig. Check.

Black silk stockings. Check.

Push-up bra. Check.

Erotic face mask. Check.

Lots and lots of condoms. Check.

Just reading over the list made her feel all warm and tingly and soft inside. This evening—during the ultraposh Boston Ladies League charity costume ball thrown annually on the Friday before Labor Day weekend—she intended on bedazzling the pants off Richard Montgomery Hancock the III.

Katie had spent her lunch hour shopping. She'd just returned to work fifteen minutes late and out of breath. Furtively, she kicked the loot farther underneath her desk, and then darted a glance over her shoulder to see if her boss had noticed her tardiness.

"What didja buy?" asked her office mate, Tanisha Taylor, as she sauntered through the door, grande soy latte in hand.

Katie shrugged. "Nothing much."

At five-nine, Tanisha towered over Katie's own five feet three inches. They were both twenty-four and they'd started working as graphic artists at Sharper Designs on the very same day ten months earlier. It was the longest Katie had ever worked anywhere and she was starting to feel the strain of being in one place too long.

With her radiant, caramel complexion and deep chocolate-brown eyes, Tanisha was drop-dead beautiful. She wore her hair in a tightly braided shoulder-length style that made her narrow face look even thinner. She possessed the lean muscular build of a dancer, quite the opposite of Katie's well-rounded, non-athletic figure. They made for an unusual looking pair.

Today her coworker was dressed in a lavender blouse made of pure silk that she wore tucked into a pair of straight-legged, black slacks and sensible black flats. But Katie knew from the wild nights they'd recently spent closing down bars that beneath the buttoned-down attire lurked the adventuresome soul of a Nubian goddess.

Tanisha spied the red-and-black striped bag from Fetching Fantasies and dove for it before Katie could block her. Tanisha set down her latte, perched on the edge of Katie's desk and peeked inside the bag.

"Oo-la-la, what have we here? *Parlez-vous français?*" she teased.

Katie snatched the bag away and clutched it to her chest. "Just a costume for the Ladies League masquerade party. No biggie."

Tanisha grinned. "You are going to be the hussy of the ball in that getup."

"That's the general idea."

"Spill it. Who've you got lined up in your crosshairs?"

Returning Tanisha's sly grin, Katie slowly shook her head.

"Don't give me that. I know you've got something up your sleeve."

Katie tilted her head, lowered her eyelashes and slanted Tanisha a sideways glance. "Do you know Richard Hancock?"

"Everyone in town knows Richard. What are you trying to do? Ruffle all the blue-blood feathers in Boston?"

That comment pulled her up short. Why did she suddenly feel as if her conscience were the target and Tanisha's accusation a straight flying arrow?

Bull's-eye.

"What makes you say that?"

"Why else would you want to hook up with Richard 'The Dick' Hancock? He's *sooo* not your type." Tanisha hopped off Katie's desk and plopped down in front of her drafting board.

"What do you mean? Richard is a very handsome guy."

"I'm not talking about his looks."

"What's wrong with Richard?"

"Nothing is wrong with Richard. What's wrong is that you're plotting to seduce him at the Ladies League ball." Tanisha clicked her tongue.

"What's so bad about that?"

"Face it, Katie. You've got a knack for causing a stir."

"I don't."

"You do."

"How so?"

"Who got caught kissing the CEO's son under the mistletoe at the office Christmas party, hmm?"

"Hey," Katie said defensively. "How was I supposed to know he'd just gotten engaged?"

"That's my point, K. You don't always take the time to ask the right questions and it often lands you in hot water. Subconsciously, I think you enjoy causing a scandal."

"I do not." Did she?

"Either that or you're into self-sabotage. Which is it?"

"Neither."

"If you say so." Tanisha sounded skeptical.

"I say so."

"And the Nile is just a river in Egypt." Tanisha snorted.

Was she sabotaging herself? As the youngest of three sisters growing up in a household run by their loving mother and strict naval-officer father, Katie had done a little acting out for attention, but so what?

She'd played hooky a few times in high school. Once

or twice, she'd gotten caught sneaking out her bedroom window to meet a boyfriend. She enjoyed making Great-Aunt Josephine's upper-crust nose wrinkle in disapproval by listening to hip-hop, using street slang and wearing jeans to family gatherings. Honestly, she'd never done anything too radical. Katie just liked having fun. Her motives were no more complicated than a Cyndi Lauper song.

Well, okay, maybe sometimes it got stifling with her two older, oh-so-perfect sisters. Brooke was the beautiful caregiver, Joey the smart go-getter and they were both as good as gold. By default, that left Katie with the title of wild child. But everyone had a family label, right? And she chose to wear hers proudly.

To be honest, even after their father had passed away five years ago, she and her sisters had still lived a fairy-tale life. They'd been lucky, blessed, until this past year when their world had totally collapsed.

Katie didn't want to think about it, but the rush of memories overwhelmed her and she felt herself caught in a tornado of emotion that squeezed the breath from her lungs. She forced a smile, determined not to let Tanisha know about the sorrow knotting up inside her.

But a smile couldn't stop the sad feelings.

In January, Katie and her sisters had received the horrible news that their beloved mother, Daisy, had been diagnosed with pancreatic cancer. Katie denied it for as long as she could. She'd pretended it was all a big mistake, that their mother was fine. But each day Daisy Winfield grew weaker and sicker until Katie could deny it no longer.

After that, she'd gotten angry. When Brooke had told

her that she was stuck in the second stage of grief, the comment had pissed her off. Sainted Brooke, who never did anything wrong apparently leapfrogged right over the five stages of grief. She'd quickly skimmed from denial to anger to depression and bargaining straight on through to acceptance.

Katie, according to Brooke, had never gotten past anger.

Maybe she hadn't. But how was she supposed to get past it? Her mother had only been fifty-three when she passed away in July, only four months after she'd been diagnosed. There hadn't been nearly enough time to say goodbye.

It wasn't fair.

Katie closed her eyes and inhaled sharply at the pain of remembering that awful night when their mother had died.

She'd been restless, feverish and babbling about a lost baby. Daisy had clutched her daughters' hands and begged them to find the baby girl. They had no idea what baby she was talking about. The hospice nurse had assured them it was just the effects of the heavy pain medication she was on, but it had been upsetting to see her mother so distressed during her last minutes on Earth.

Involuntarily, Katie laid a hand across her heart and felt a solid ache for the loss of her mother.

"Katie?" Tanisha's voice snapped her out of the past and back into the present.

She opened her eyes.

Tanisha had an odd expression on her face. She canted her head and a dark braid fell against her chiseled cheekbone. "Are you all right?"

"Uh-huh."

"You don't look all right."

"I am."

Tanisha nodded at the shopping bags crammed underneath Katie's desk. "Does this shopping spree and Ladies League seduction, and other crazy behavior have anything to do with losing your mother?"

Her coworker was more perceptive than she imagined. Tanisha's party-girl personality gave the impression that she wasn't the type to pry into people's deep, dark secrets, which was probably one of the reasons Katie had been drawn to her. Katie herself was not a fan of digging into her own psyche.

"Why would you think that?" Katie forced a laugh, but it came out sounding strangled and strange.

"I was thinking that maybe you're looking to seduce Richard as a way of drowning your sorrow. You know, choking out the pain with pleasure."

"No, no. Of course not. That's ludicrous. I can't believe you thought that."

"This coming weekend is the two-month anniversary of your mother's death."

"So?"

"So maybe instead of facing what's upsetting you, you're seducing Richard Hancock."

"Well, I'm not," Katie snapped.

Tanisha held up her palms. "Oookay, I was merely checking. No need to get testy."

"I don't understand. What do you have against me hooking up with Richard?"

"He's just not what you need right now."

"Why not?" she asked. "He's fun and flirts and likes to have a good time."

"Exactly."

"Meaning?" ·

"You're two of a kind."

"Again, why is that a problem?"

"Come on, be straight with me, do you even like Richard?"

Katie shrugged. "Sure."

"What do you like about him?" Tanisha lifted a finger. "And you can't say anything physical."

"He's…he's…"

Why couldn't she think of what she liked about Richard beside his thick blond hair and his radiant white-toothed smile and his big, broad tanned hands? He wasn't terribly bright, nor was he horribly reliable. But come on, she wasn't talking about marrying the guy. She just needed to get laid.

"Can't do it, can you?"

"He's funny."

"No, you're the funny one. He laughs at *your* jokes."

"Really?"

"Really."

Oops! Tanisha was right, but Katie didn't want to admit it. "Okay, then that's what I like about him. He makes me feel funny."

"Funny ha-ha or funny weird?"

"Now you're just giving me a hard time. What's the deal?"

Tanisha took a deep breath. "Let's drop the conversation. We've both got work to wrap up before the holiday weekend."

"No, seriously, I want to know."

"You sure?" Tanisha arched an eyebrow. "You promise not to get mad at me?"

"What do you mean? I'm not an angry person."

"You didn't used to be," Tanisha said.

"But I am now?"

"Well, sometimes, kind of, ever since your mother passed away."

That stunned her. To hear it from Brooke was one thing. As the oldest, Brooke had often seen it as her job to monitor Katie and correct her behavior, but to hear it from her friend was another story.

"It's okay," Tanisha offered. "Everyone understands. You've been through a lot. But instead of hooking up with good-time guys like Richard, you might be at a point in your life where it's time you checked out the other side of the fence. Maybe you should try being with someone more substantial."

"I don't get it. Where is this coming from? You party and flirt as much as I do."

"Yeah, but since I've started dating Dwayne I'm looking at things a bit differently."

"Don't tell me that you and Dwayne are getting serious! You've only known him what? A month? And he lives in Denver. It's easy to have a great relationship when you rarely see each other."

"We're not talking about me and Dwayne. We're talking about you, and I think you're doing this as some kind of rebellion you never outgrew. Deep down inside, you're a lot more traditional than you want people to believe."

"Huh?"

"If you want to party and flirt and have lots of casual sex then great, do it. Don't apologize for it. But if you're doing it simply to prove to yourself that you're not like the rest of your family, maybe you should take a second look at what kind of lifestyle will really make you happy."

"This is ridiculous."

"Is it?"

"Winfield," boomed a gruff voice from the across the room.

Katie swiveled in her chair to see her boss, Max Kruger, standing in the doorway. A persistent frown rode his bushy eyebrows. Max was fiftyish, sported an out-of-style crew cut and had a penchant for wearing chinos with crisply starched white shirts. He looked like a basketball coach and managed his employees with the same sort of affable crustiness.

"Yes, Mr. Kruger?"

File in hand, Max strode into their office.

"You're going to have to stay late tonight."

"But it's the Friday before the holiday weekend," Katie said, feeling her plans for seduction slipping away. All she'd wanted was to end the evening in bed with Richard. She'd been dreaming about the feel of a masculine arm around her waist, the smell of a man's scent in her nostrils, the sweet oblivion of an orgasm.

"So?"

"I have plans."

"Do you like your job, Winfield?"

"Yes, sir."

Max thrust the file at her. "Then you're staying late. Kringle's Krackers didn't like the color fill on the logo. They want something more urban chic."

"For overpriced saltines?"

"Hey, it's what the customer wants." He paused before delivering the really bad news. "And you've got to come up with the new palette by Tuesday. They need it right away for a special promo venture they have planned." Max turned and stalked from the room.

Katie groaned and swiveled her chair to face her computer. Muttering darkly under her breath, she grabbed the Kringle's Krackers file.

"Maybe you should look at this as a sign," Tanisha said.

"What do you mean?"

"That you're not supposed to seduce Richard Hancock at the Ladies League masquerade ball."

She paused a moment, giving Tanisha's suggestion some thought. "I could look at it as a sign," she said. "Or I could take it as a challenge to see how quickly I can get this project fixed and get over there."

Tanisha shook her head. "I gotta hand it to you, K. Whenever you put your mind to something, you put your mind to it."

"Nah." Katie grinned. "I'm just deeply into self-sabotage."

The earthy smell of impending autumn hung thick on the evening breeze. Katie hustled from the Sharper Designs offices, nestled among other quaint structures in an older area of Boston not far from downtown.

At the turn of the twentieth century, the stately buildings had once been personal residences. Then in the 1970s, the area had been zoned commercial and most of the families had pulled up stakes and moved on, leaving their homes to be converted into offices by enterprising developers. The renovated homes created a cozy work environment, but parking space was at a premium and the nearest parking lot lay three blocks away.

It was almost 9:00 p.m. and the Ladies League ball would be in full swing. The streetlamps glowed hazy against the dreamy mist of fog rolling in from the harbor. Katie hurried down the street, her arms laden with the packages she'd bought on her lunch hour.

Her stilettos tapped smartly against the cement sidewalk. Underneath her light fall coat, she wore the French-maid costume. Not wanting to waste time by going home, she'd dressed at the office. She felt decidedly naughty and that naughtiness escalated her excitement and strengthened her resolve.

Come hell or high water, she was determined to seduce Richard Hancock.

Feeling both nervous and brave, walking the streets alone in her costume, she took a deep fortifying breath. What would Richard think of her outfit? She hadn't told him what she was wearing because the French-maid getup was a spur-of-the-moment decision. Richard, however, had promised to come as Jack Sparrow from *Pirates of the Caribbean,* complete with a Johnny Depp booty pirate's wig. Pirate and captive was her favorite sexual fantasy.

Katie could hardly wait. The thrill of the chase quickened her pulse.

She scurried past the pet store that had just opened up the week before. Muted low-level lighting was on in the building and as she turned to step off the curb, she spotted him.

Her heart hammered and her breath caught. Her gaze met his and she was a goner.

The puppy, a honey-colored cocker spaniel, was caged inside the window. His big, sweet chocolate-brown eyes locked on hers.

"Oh." She breathed, changed directions and walked back toward him. "Oh, you are too cute."

Frantically, he wagged his tail.

In that instant Katie fell in love. *How much is that doggy in the window?* The song ran through her head.

You with a dog? Ha!

It was a laughable idea. She lived in a condo and was rarely home. Plus, she'd never had a pet, although she had always wanted one. She remembered begging for a puppy as a kid, but her parents had told her she was too irresponsible. She couldn't even keep her room clean; how could they trust her to feed and walk a pet?

Katie pleaded with her mom and dad. They'd resisted. She made lavish promises. They balked. She found a stray and fed him cheesy puffs from her lunch to get him to follow her home. Their maid had called the animal shelter.

Finally, realizing how determined she was, her father had relented. He told her if she could prove she was responsible enough to take care of an animal, then she could have one. His test consisted of Katie caring for an egg as if it were a puppy.

She had to take the egg with her wherever she went,

making sure never to leave it behind. Keeping track of that egg had been darned hard for an eight-year-old, but after two weeks without a misstep, she was picking out names for her puppy.

Then on the last day, Katie ran to greet her father at the front door as he returned home from work, the egg clutched in her hand. In her excitement, she'd tripped and fallen. Splattering the egg across the foyer in a vivid yellow splash of yolk.

She'd been inconsolable. Her parents were right. She was too irresponsible for a puppy.

Her stern yet loving father didn't hold the accidental egg smash against her. He'd taken her to the nearest pet store and let her pick out the dog of her choice.

She had selected an exuberant cocker spaniel exactly like this one. Same honey-colored coat, same chocolate-brown eyes. She had named the puppy Duke. It had been the happiest day of her eight-year-old life.

Then she'd gotten Duke home and Brooke had immediately started sneezing. Her sister sneezed all through the weekend, her eyes swelling up, and her nose running. Daisy had taken Brooke to the doctor the next day and they'd returned home with the news that Brooke was highly allergic to dogs.

Katie had been forced to give Duke away. Even now, sixteen years later, she still felt the awful punch to her stomach when she thought about it.

"Hey, little guy," she cooed, and crouched down to the puppy's eye level and put her hand to the window front. He tried to lick her fingers, his pink tongue rubbing wetly against the glass.

From past experience, she knew that if she scooped him up in her arms his fur would feel soft as doll hair and he'd lick her face until she ended up on the floor giggling breathlessly while he nibbled at her ears.

Her stomach clutched. A mixture of emotions melded inside her—tenderness, regret and lingering irritation with her sister Brooke's allergies because she had been forced to miss out on the joys of puppy ownership. Petty maybe, but it was how she felt.

You could have a puppy now.

No, it was too late to relive her childhood. There was no room in her busy life for a dog. Maybe someday, but not now.

"Gotta go," she whispered, rising to her feet and waving goodbye. "There's a party waiting and I've got a gorgeous man to seduce."

The puppy whimpered and the wagging of his tail slowed. He sensed she was about to leave him.

"It's better this way, truly. You wouldn't be happy at my place. You'd be cooped up all day by yourself. It wouldn't be fair to you. I'm only thinking of your best interest."

The cocker spaniel stared at her with his big, adoring eyes.

Her heart ripped. This was silly. What was the matter with her? Getting sentimental over a dog. He was adorable. Someone else would buy him. She had no reason to feel guilty.

But somehow, she did.

She had to shake this feeling, had to shrug off the sadness weighing down her shoulders. Had to stop thinking about her mother and Duke, the puppy she'd only had for a weekend, and Tanisha's eerily accurate assessment of her.

Fun.

That was what she needed. A strong drink, loud music, a roomful of people dressed in colorful costumes.

And a man to seduce who wouldn't look at her in the morning the way this puppy was looking at her now.

Head down, she rushed away, trying her very best to outpace the mental demons with which she had no desire to wrestle. She was going to that party and she wasn't about to let anyone or anything keep her from seducing her pirate.

2

FOR MOST of his adult life, Liam James had been all about the job. Nothing mattered more to him than the real-estate company he'd built from the ground up and molded into a multimillion-dollar empire by the time he was thirty.

He loved his work and excelled in a crisis. It was the worrying beforehand and afterwards that did him in. He was always on the lookout for trouble. And in an odd way he was relieved when it came.

Troubleshooting was what he knew. Lack of trouble made him uneasy. Edgy anticipation. That was his true nemesis. It threw him off his game.

And he was feeling edgy tonight.

Especially since he was dressed in this ridiculous *Pirates of the Caribbean*, Jack Sparrow costume. By the time he'd made it over to the costume-rental place, this was the only disguise left in his size. He'd already spotted three other Jack Sparrows at the party. Apparently the costume-supply companies had gone overboard on the pirate theme this year.

"What the hell am I doing here?" he muttered under his breath, and scanned the collected crowd at the Ladies League charity masquerade party.

The expensively decorated ballroom was filled with ultrathin, cosmetically enhanced women and self-important, overfed rich men in lavish costumes. The kind of highbrow shindig Liam loathed.

The question was rhetorical. He already knew the answer.

He was here to get an up close and personal look at the man whose seed had spawned him. The man who'd never acknowledged him, nor sent his mother one penny of child support beyond the three hundred dollars he had thrown at her thirty-two years ago, when he'd told her to get an abortion.

That man was Boston's incumbent mayor, Finn Delancy. Who was up for reelection and was pegged to win it by a landslide.

For years, Liam had imagined this meeting. The moment when he introduced himself and told him, "Thanks for nothing, you worthless son of a bitch. My mother and I made it fine without you. And FYI, blue blood or not, I can buy and sell your ass three times over."

But now that he was here, and it was the moment of truth, Liam wasn't sure exactly how to go about it.

The mayor wore a cowboy costume—ten gallon hat, spurs that jangled, leather chaps, the whole nine yards. He looked utterly foolish but that didn't stop a bevy of beautiful young women from collecting around him like bargain shoppers to a fire sale.

According to Liam's mother, Jeanine, Finn had more sexual charisma than Bill Clinton and JFK all rolled into one. He gritted his teeth and fisted his hands. Personally, he couldn't see the appeal.

"Something the matter, boss?" asked Liam's right-hand man, Tony Gregory. Tony was dressed as one of the band members from KISS and damn if he didn't look seriously freaky. Not at all like his normal affable self. "You seem uptight."

Liam gave a sharp shake of his head. "Nothing's wrong."

"So tell me again why I'm here?" Tony cocked his head and sent Liam an assessing gaze.

"My date and I decided it was better if we just stayed friends, so she's not coming tonight. I had the extra ticket." He couldn't really call her his girlfriend. They'd only gone out a few times. "There's no sense letting two hundred dollars go to waste."

What he didn't tell his most trusted confidant was that he badly needed moral support. Willingly admitting a weakness wasn't something he did, not even to himself. He'd known Tony since their days at Harvard School of Business, but he'd never told him his deepest secret—that he was the bastard son of one of the most influential men in Boston high society.

"You lost another one?" Tony whistled. "Damn, and I really liked Brooke."

"Don't worry. We're still friends."

"What the hell do you do to chase off so many chicks? You're rich, good-looking and you bathe regularly. Why don't any of them stick around for more than a few dates? What gives?"

"I have a low tolerance for the frivolous," Liam said, narrowing his eyes at Finn Delancy, who had just planted a kiss on the hand of a giggling starlet.

"You're a workaholic is what you are, and women hate coming second to a man's career."

"True enough."

"Did you like her?"

"Of course I liked her."

"But you didn't like her enough to make an effort to keep her?"

"We both realized we're too much alike. And while Brooke is very pretty, there was no strong sexual spark between us. Plus, she told me she needed a man who could give her his undivided attention and I'm sorry—" he shrugged "—that's not me. Work always comes first."

Tony stared at him, mouth dropping open in amazement. "So…you've never been in love."

Liam shifted his weight, crossed his arms over his chest. "What makes you say that?"

"When a woman gets under your skin fully and completely, then you'll willingly give up everything to be with her."

"Everything?"

"Everything." Tony nodded sagely, his ebony KISS wig bobbing about his shoulders.

"If that's your definition of love, then I'm glad I've never been there."

"It's how I feel about Jess. She's the most important thing in the world to me," he said, an ardent expression on his face. "Nothing comes before her. Ever."

"Not even your job as my VP?"

"Nope." Tony shook his head.

"You're serious."

"As a heart attack."

"Still? Even after five years of marriage?"

"She fascinates me more each day. She's my lover, my companion, my best friend."

Liam snorted in disbelief. It was sad, but true. He'd never been in love, had never met any woman who fascinated him more than his work.

Although, he'd thought he was in love once, during his sophomore year in college, with Arianna Baxter, a high-society beauty. They'd been study partners, and he'd hoped for more but never had the courage to ask her out. Her family was so wealthy, and he was so poor. Then she'd invited him to a lavish sorority party and his hopes had soared. Except when he got there, he discovered the joke was on him. It was a "pauper party," where the sorority sisters dared each other to bring the poorest, most socially unacceptable guy they could find. The kicker was that Arianna won first prize for bringing him.

"How come you keep staring at Mayor Delaney?" Tony asked.

"I'm thinking maybe I should go introduce myself to him."

"He'll just hit you up for a campaign contribution," Tony remarked.

I'd love the chance to tell him where he could stick his request for money.

"He can ask. I don't have to give it."

Tony glanced over his shoulder at the mayor. "You've got your competition cut out for you, dude. Delancy's surrounded."

"Yeah, but I'll figure it out. Get to schmoozing, Gregory. We're here for the business contacts."

"Actually, I came for the free food. Much as I love her, my Jess isn't much of a cook."

"So schmooze the buffet. I'll catch up with you later," Liam said, and then started across the crowded room, his glare beaded on the mayor.

The closer he got, the harder his heart thumped. This was the man who'd charmed Liam's seventeen-year-old mother, bedded her, and then left her pregnant and heartbroken. He'd denied his paternity and waltzed glibly back to his wife. All the old resentment that had been seething in Liam since childhood fisted into a knot of pure hatred.

Revenge. The dish best served cold.

And he was about to dine.

Liam had the speech prepared. He had been practicing it over and over in his head for years. Waiting for the moment when his financial success eclipsed Finn Delancy's. Waiting for the slam dunk. The one thing he'd never envisioned was giving his speech dressed as a pirate, but what the hell? It seemed fitting.

Every bigwig in Boston—not to mention a nice collection of reporters from the media—was in attendance at the party. His goal was to shame and embarrass the hell out of Delancy in the most public of forums.

And the Ladies League ball—the biggest charity event of the social season—definitely qualified. Determined to see this thing through, Liam reached for the document burning a hole in the back pocket of his black leather Jack Sparrow pants.

It was his birth certificate.

"Mayor Delancy," Liam said and thrust himself through the circle of women surrounding his father.

Delancy swung his gaze around to fix on him. The man's eyes were the same color of hazel as Liam's own. They also shared the same jawline—strong, hard, resolute. "What can I do for you, son?"

Son.

The word hung in the air weighed with a meaning only Liam understood. But soon, very soon, Finn Delancy would understand it, as well, and so would his enamored constituents. What would they think of their illustrious leader then?

"For you," Liam ground out, and thrust the folded birth certificate at Delancy. He had to clench his teeth to keep his emotions in check so that his hand wouldn't tremble and give away his barely cloaked rage.

Delancy stared at him a moment, clearly confused. The celebutante at the mayor's elbow tittered for no discernable reason. Liam stood there with the folded piece of paper held outstretched at arm's length.

"Oh," Delancy blinked. "Gotcha."

The hell you do. I'm the one who's got you.

Delancy reached in the front pocket of his cowboy vest. Going for his reading glasses? Liam guessed.

But the mayor did not extract a reading-glass case. Rather, he pulled out an expensive ballpoint pen and accepted the folded document.

"Turn around," the mayor said.

"What?"

"Turn around?"

Liam was so surprised by the request he found himself complying and felt Delancy rest the birth certificate against his shoulder blade, using his back as a support while he scrawled something on the paper.

What the hell?

"Here you go," Delancy said, proudly.

Liam turned back around, his shoulder tingling from the touch of the man he'd hated for more years than he could count. Delancy slapped the birth certificate into his palm as two burly bodyguards stepped forward.

"Mayor," said bodyguard number one, "your limousine has arrived."

"Excuse me." Delancy flashed Liam an artificial smile. "I have another engagement."

Bodyguard Number Two took the mayor by the elbow and led him away through the crowd. At the same time Bodyguard Number One gave his arm to the celebutante. It didn't take a rocket scientist to figure out with whom the mayor would be spending the rest of the evening.

Confused by what had just happened, Liam stared down at the folded birth certificate in his hand.

There, written in Delancy's shaky scrawl were words that sent shame, anger, embarrassment and hatred shooting through Liam's veins.

It's always nice to meet a fan. Best wishes, Finn Delancy.

Liam's lungs constricted, and he found it hard to breathe. His hand was trembling now from pure rage that no amount of teeth clenching could abate.

An autograph!

The low-life, egotistical, jackass had just autographed his illegitimate son's birth certificate.

By the time Katie arrived at the Hightower mansion where this year's Ladies League masquerade ball was being held, the crowd was at maximum capacity. Even in three-inch stilettos, she still had to stand on tiptoe to see above the costumed throng packed into the foyer and snaking out through the grand hallway.

Waiters squeezed through the mob, balancing silver trays laden with flutes of fizzy champagne. The music was so loud she could barely think, and the hum of hundreds of voices was even louder.

Where was Richard?

For one brief moment, she thought about going home, but then quickly reconsidered, recalling how much money she'd spent on this seduction. She reached for a glass of champagne from the tray of a passing waiter and took a big swallow to ward off her building nervousness.

The decadently arousing song "Ooh La La" by the British group Goldfrapp came over the speakers, oozing glam sex with a throbbing bass. She found herself twitching her hips in time to the seductive tune and scanning the crowd for anyone she knew.

But the disguises had done their jobs. She recognized no one. Feeling giddy at the weirdness of all her friends looking like strangers, she finished off the champagne and set her empty glass on a nearby table.

Body tingling with taboo sensations, Katie winnowed around Spider-Man chatting up Cleopatra, slipped past Mickey Mantle talking about the New England Patriots with Elvis Presley and then put a hand to her waist-long auburn wig to make sure it was still on straight.

The eyeholes of the wide mask that covered more than half her face were too narrow and she was having problems seeing much of anything in her peripheral vision. It was stifling hot, even though there wasn't much to her costume, with so many people sardined into the room.

She looked for a side exit. Maybe Richard had stepped outside for some fresh air. It might take her an hour to find him in this madhouse.

Disheartened, she settled her shoulder against the doorjamb leading into the room where the buffet was laid out. The next time another waiter circled in front of her, she reached for a second glass of champagne.

Could Richard have already left the party?

For the first time she noticed that men were brazenly staring at her. Lots of men, in fact.

Katie took a quick peak down at her costume. Good gosh. When she'd dressed so hurriedly at Sharper Designs she hadn't realized exactly how low the neckline dipped. Her cleavage was practically spilling out of her dress.

Flustered, she crossed her arms over her chest and turned away from the buffet line, only to find more ogling men. She hurried into the ballroom, heart thumping with anxious excitement.

Apparently a French-maid was every man's fantasy.

She was accustomed to masculine attention, but not this intense. Men with cloaked identities lusting after her.

Where was Richard?

Tanisha was right. Pursuing Richard at the party was a bad idea. Go home.

"Don't panic," Katie muttered under her breath. "This is a costume party. They don't recognize you any more than you recognize them."

And then that's when she saw him.

Mayor Delancy sweeping through the crowd with his bodyguards, headed toward the front door. Even in his cowboy costume it was impossible to miss the larger-than-life mayor.

But standing in the mayor's wake was the man she'd been searching for. The very Caribbean pirate she'd come here to seduce.

Resentment pummeled Liam's stomach like a heavyweight boxer finishing off his wobbly-kneed opponent. Reflexively, he curled his fist around the birth certificate autographed by his biological father. The desire to punch something was so strong he could taste it.

Raw, bitter, black.

For the last twelve years he'd worked toward this moment, worked and waited, and Delancy had pulled the rug right out from under him. What should he do now?

You'll go at him again. You picked the wrong time, the wrong place, that's all.

His mother had never wanted him to do this. She was happy now, married to a great guy and living on a farm in upstate New York. She thought he should just forget about Finn Delancy and be proud of everything he'd accomplished without his old man's help.

But it wasn't that simple for Liam. He couldn't let it go. Anger twisted him up inside. The place was filled with privileged blue bloods, no doubt many of whom thought they could treat people any way they wanted and get away with it.

Liam blazed a hard gaze around the room. Frivolous, pampered rich people throwing silly costume parties. If they really wanted to give to charity, just write a check and don't waste money on lavish celebrations.

You're richer than most of them.

Yes, but he'd gotten his money the hard way. He'd earned every penny of it, not had it handed to him on a platinum platter.

Adrenaline, anger and frustration coursed through him. He needed to dissipate these feelings. Needed to get a firm grip on his emotions. Exercise. He needed exercise. A run in the park never failed to give him back his sense of control.

He had to get the hell out of here.

But then something caught his eye that made Liam forget everything except the fact he hadn't had sex in almost a year.

There, on the other side of the ballroom, stood a gorgeous vixen in a French maid costume and she was staring straight at him, as if he were the man of her most forbidden midnight fantasies.

Coyly, she tossed her auburn wig.

Liam drove his hand through his own wig.

She licked her lips.

Drawing in a ragged breath, he hooked his thumbs through his belt loop.

Her eyes widened, and he saw a telltale red flush spread from her generous cleavage up her long slender throat.

His body hardened and he shifted, widening his stance, pointing his boots in her direction.

She lowered her eyelashes, dropped her hands. His gaze fell to the creamy inside of her wrist, and then tracked up her smooth, delicate skin to her shoulders. She peeked at him again and then slyly winked. Even with the barrier of her black mask cloaking most of her face, he was absolutely certain she was winking at him.

Boldly, Liam winked back.

Why the hell not? Sex was better than jogging for blowing off steam and after what had happened before with Delancy, he could certainly do with the distraction.

And she was one fine distraction with those shapely legs encased in lust-arousing black fishnet stockings. He could easily imagine himself tugging that silky material over the curve of her calf.

She angled him a long, lingering look.

He caught it, held it.

Quickly, she looked away again, but there was no mistaking her invitation.

Come play with me.

His blood revved hot.

She turned and walked away.

The thundering in his veins intensified. Curiosity grabbed him by the short hairs and hung on tight. Who was this mysterious woman? Did he know her? Something about her seemed vaguely familiar, but he couldn't put his finger on what it was.

She made her way through the crowd, hips rolling seductively, as aloof as the blue-blooded princess she undoubtedly was. When she got to the doorway, she paused. Her long fingers stroked the door casing as she tossed him a glance over her shoulder. She looked damned provocative, even in a room chock-full of people dressed in suggestive garb.

Follow me, her eyes whispered.

Normally, Liam wasn't the type of guy who allowed his libido to overrule his common sense. But he was horny and desperately needing something to salve his battered ego, and she was hot and willing.

Why not go for it?

You shouldn't let your anger at Delancy drive you to casual sex with a frisky member of the Ladies League simply to prove you can bed the social elite.

Maybe not, but his gaze was ensnared on her full, rich mouth that was clearly made for kissing. She pursed her lips, slowly blew him a kiss and then crooked her index finger.

This way.

Liam felt the impact of the gesture slam low in his groin. Simultaneously, hormones and endorphins lit up both his body and his brain. He gulped against the sheer force of the sensation. This French maid wanted to have some fun. Why shouldn't he be the one to accommodate her?

He shook his head. What kind of spell had she cast over him? His tongue was cemented to the roof of his mouth.

His eyes were transfixed by her lithe form. His nose twitched, suddenly sensitized to the scent of seduction in the air. His ears filled with a blinding white roaring noise.

She strutted off a second time.

Mesmerized, he watched her hips sway.

Liam went all Neanderthal then and lumbered after her. *Must have woman.*

By the time he reached where she'd been standing, she was already in the archway of another room. The place could have been completely empty. That's how unaware he was of the crowd jostling around them.

The French maid paused again, but this time she did not look back. Apparently, she'd assumed he would follow.

She was correct.

Sending her auburn curls bouncing over her shoulders with a toss of her head, she turned to the right and started down a long corridor.

Liam made a beeline after her.

People were all around him, talking, laughing, joking, drinking, but he could have been stranded on a deserted island or trapped in a timeless vortex. He was that focused on Miss French Maid's fanny as she slipped through the costumed throng.

She winnowed around a man the size of a boxcar dressed like Paul Bunyan and Liam couldn't see her anymore. He quickened his pace, but at the next doorway, Paul Bunyan turned, blocking his path.

"Excuse me." Liam stepped to his right.

Paul Bunyan moved in the same direction at the exact same moment.

Liam corrected, angling to the left.

So did Bunyan.

Was this on purpose? What was happening here? Liam frowned.

"Shall we dance?" Paul Bunyan chuckled, and Liam realized he'd been unnecessarily suspicious. By the time he got around the guy, he found himself faced with a long hallway filled with doors. His French maid had vanished.

"Dammit," he muttered.

It's all for the best. He was feeling much too vulnerable to be indulging in anonymous sex. That kind of solace, while great in the moment, wouldn't fix anything. It wouldn't make up for the aching for a real father that had dogged his bones since he was a kid.

He stood there in the corridor, staring at the doors, wondering if she was behind one, not wanting to leave in case she reappeared. A minute ticked past. And then another.

Face it. She's gone.

He turned to retrace his steps when suddenly the door behind him opened and a hand reached out to grab him by the scruff of his collar.

Long, manicured fingernails tickled the back of his neck and the next thing Liam knew, he was being hauled into a pitch black closet.

The French maid wrapped her arms around him and covered his face in kisses. At least he hoped it was the French maid.

She murmured something in French. He didn't understand the language, but he did get the gist of her suggestive message. He tried to take a step back to clear his head, but her fingers were frantically working the buttons of his puffy white pirate shirt.

"Slow down," he said, or rather tried to say. His throat was twisted so tight with need the sounds came out as scarcely more than an excited groan.

Her mind-boggling aroma, which smelled like a cross between apricots and stargazer lilies, filled his nose and shot up his desire. He could see absolutely nothing in the darkness, but the rest of his senses were fully attuned and ready to be indulged.

"What…how…who…" He wrenched out the words, unable to form a coherent thought.

"Shh." She placed an index finger over his lips. Her skin tasted forbidden.

He thought of truffles and Russian caviar and saffron, the most expensive spice in the world. His nerve endings blazed. In the back of his mind, far off in the distance, sounding as if it had been locked up in a dry, dusty trunk for centuries, his muffled conscience tried to get his attention.

Hey, sport, this seems awfully odd. Sexy babe coming on to you, no strings attached. You know there's always strings attached. Something's wrong. Pull your head out of the hormone soup. Think this through. Last thing you want is to be like your old man. Hey, hey…

His scruples got no further because his brain short-circuited, closing off everything except the exquisite glory of her hot little mouth on his.

3

KATIE COULDN'T believe she was really doing this. It felt so naughty, so wicked, so *wrong*.

And yet, it felt so damn good.

She should have known Richard would be a world-class kisser. He was one of the hottest bachelors in Boston and very popular with the ladies. Why had she waited this long to seduce him?

He seemed so receptive, so responsive. When she curled her fingers around his forearm, he actually shivered.

She was shivering, too.

His mouth was heated and moist and he tasted of peppermint. His arm went around her waist and he tilted her backward in the closet.

The sleeves of the coats on the rack swayed with their movements, the rough material of the garments brushing provocatively against her bare arms. Farther down on the rod, a couple of empty coat hangers rattled against the sway.

His breathing was as ragged and raspy as hers. The bold pirate was plunging his demanding tongue past her teeth, plundering her mouth with a brazen zeal, taking what he wanted, leaving her breathless and clinging tightly to him.

He pulled her closer, crushing her against his broad, muscular chest. The stiff short skirt of her outfit crinkled at the pressure, and her scalp tingled hotly.

Each strumming beat of her heart was a sexual question mark.

What now?

What was going to happen next?

Would he run his rough hand up her leg?

Would he give her the mind-blasting orgasm she hungered for?

"Woman." The word was dragged from his damp lips in a husky inhalation of breath. He pulled his mouth from hers and tracked his tongue down her chin to her throat. "You are so, so sexy."

She threw back her head, exposing her throat, giving him greater access to the pulse fluttering at the hollow of her neck.

Oh, he smelled good. Like candy canes and the joy of Christmas morning. She wondered what cologne he had on. Usually Richard wore a much cooler, more sophisticated fragrance.

Hmm, should she ask him?

And possibly spoil the moment? Was she nuts?

That sobering notion quickened her breathing, but it didn't scare her. And that, in itself, was terrifying.

What was wrong with her? Why was she so willing to walk the edge, to tempt fate, to push the envelope beyond common sense?

Rhetorical question. She knew the answer. Ever since her mother had died she'd felt an overwhelming need to make her emotional pain disappear.

Without Daisy as an anchor, it was as if she no longer had anything to lose. Why not gamble everything for a little fun? What was the point of holding herself in reserve?

Life was short. Live it to the fullest. That was her motto.

Thankfully, his honeyed mouth was back on hers, forcing the dark thoughts from her head, kissing her hard and deep. His wicked tongue did its job, making her forget the emotional pain inside her.

Katie allowed herself to be swept up by the headlong sensation. She refused to think. Her only desire was to feel.

She teetered on her high heels, lost her balance. They stumbled together, slamming into the back of the closet. He laughed then, a hearty, substantial laugh that made her giggle. His arm tightened around her waist.

"You okay?" he asked.

"Uh-huh."

"I like this French thing you got going on. It's very hot."

"Shh." She wanted him to stop talking and start kissing her again.

"Listen…" he said, "I don't want you to…"

"No talking," she commanded.

The costumes made their encounter that much more exciting, but their garments were getting in the way. Reaching up, she pulled off his wig, wrapped her arms around his neck and plunged her fingers through his thick hair.

Her pirate took the hint and his tongue went back to doing maddening things to her mouth and causing wicked sensation to shoot straight into the center of her sex. His leather masked rubbed against hers, creating a sensation so erotic she made a soft mewling sound low in her throat.

Yes, take me to oblivion.

He made a corresponding noise, decidedly more masculine than hers. He ground his pelvis against her pubic bone and she arched her hips, letting him know exactly what she wanted.

Blood surged through her veins in a headlong rush. The darkness was absolute, the anonymity acute. It was incredible.

He kissed her, fiercely, passionately. He tasted so good—all masculine strength and sizzling heat. Restlessly, she tossed back her head, exposing her throat to him.

"Nibble on my neck," she murmured.

The minute his sharp teeth sank lightly into the tender flesh at her hollow of her throat, she groaned with pleasure.

Quiet. She had to be quiet. People might hear. But she couldn't even think straight, much less fret about the potential for public humiliation. At this point, she didn't care.

His palms skimmed up underneath her flimsy getup, his hands scorching the bare skin of her belly.

Desire exploded into the small tight closet with them, sending Katie on a mission of frantic grappling. She snatched at his shirt, tugging and pulling. She heard buttons pop, spit to the hardwood floor with a series of soft plopping sounds.

Once his chest was exposed, she buried her face there and inhaled deeply. His chest hairs tickled her nose and she held the hem of his shirt, still clutched in the fist of her hand.

He growled.

A tiger.

She was in the dark with a tiger.

A sweet fear washed over her. A sugary terror clogging her arteries and making her gasp for more. Her entire body tingled with fear and joy and hungry, secret longing.

Her knees wobbled. Sensing her weakness, he pressed her back flat against the wall of the closet, holding her in place with his hip.

She was on fire for him. She had never wanted any man this badly.

He didn't speak.

Golden silence.

This was very good. Dark and anonymous and quiet. Nothing but heavy, excited breathing. Not hearing his voice made her feel as if he were pure fantasy and it escalated her excitement beyond anything she'd ever dreamed of.

She felt raunchy and rash and ready. This was exactly what she needed to bypass all her troubles.

Wildly, she pressed the tip of her tongue to his broad chest and licked a long path up to the hollow of his throat. He tasted like a seafaring man. Gloriously rich and salty.

She heard her own pulse thrumming through her ears and it sounded like a river rushing downstream.

His movements were measured, controlled, but at the same time relaxed and easy. His fingers were now trailing circles around her nipples, teasing them into taut peaks.

In the inkiness, in the masquerade, he was a creature of the night. Sleek and primal, sexual in a way that quickened her breath and slicked her palms, along with other, more feminine parts of her anatomy.

The stagnant air in the closet was heavy with the sound of their rough, synchronized breathing. It smelled of the musk from their throbbing bodies. It tasted twisted and taboo.

Who—she found herself thinking in the short gaps between utter delight—*are you?*

She told herself it was Richard. It had to be Richard. Who else could it be?

Her mind thrilled to the possibilities. Why did she find the idea of a masked stranger so compelling? Why did she suddenly want him *not* to be Richard?

Was she losing her mind? Had she lost it already? Slipping over the edge of reason in a smoking-hot French-maid uniform?

He kissed her again, the glide of his tongue smooth and perfect.

Her blood moved recklessly through her. There was that thrill again, rolling like an electrical storm. Searing and stark and scary.

The pirate growled again, low and guttural. The sound vibrated through her, set her nerve endings flaming, causing her hips to twitch involuntarily and the deep folds of her moist sex to burn for him.

He unzipped her costume and slipped it off her shoulders in the darkness. Then he unhooked her bra, exposing her bare breasts. The pirate lowered his head and began to sweetly suckle one of her aching nipples while lightly pinching the other between his thumb and index finger.

The synthetic material of his fake beard tickled her skin.

Something inside of her slipped, a ship freed from its moorings, set adrift at sea. She reached up to plane his face with her hand, feeling the solid jut of his cheekbone against her palm.

His mouth was skillful. Gentle when she needed him to be, firm when she needed that, too. This pirate was taking his time.

While Katie appreciated his unanticipated leisure, at the same time it added to her anxiety. The longer this took, the more likely they were to be caught.

And that sent a fresh set of brand-new thrills and chills chasing up her spine.

His arms were strong, comforting. Oddly, in spite of the unconventional circumstances, she felt safe. She wished it wasn't so dark, wished she could see his face.

What, and spoil the fantasy?

He reached down and, grabbing one of her legs, lifted it up and cocked her heel against his hip. Katie felt her stocking being stripped away. He peeled off her stiletto. Let it clatter to the floor. Carefully, he let her leg drop, then repeated the process with her other leg.

She'd intended this encounter to be a clothes-on quickie, but it wasn't turning out that way. He wasn't playing his part how she'd imagined.

His breath on her bare skin was deep and rich— black velvet. Nimbly, his fingers worked, tickling her skin. She giggled against the lightness of his touch, the freedom it unwound in her.

Soon, she was standing with her back against the wall wearing nothing but black silk panties.

"You don't have to get undressed," she said, taking

care to keep her voice disguised, to keep the fantasy going. "We should make this fast. In case someone comes looking for us. We don't want to get caught doing the nasty at the Ladies League ball."

"Why not?" he said rough and low. "It's the perfect high-society sacrilege."

She frowned. What did he mean by that? She wished she could see his face.

The room was ebony. Only the light from underneath the crack in the door penetrated the darkness.

He said nothing, but she heard the quiet whisper of his zipper sliding down.

She sucked in her breath.

Wet heat gushed through her body. The muscles deep within her pelvis tightened. Her heart beat faster and she surprised herself by how quickly she grew slick.

His hand was a hot pressure as he reached out to trail it across the soft silk between her legs. He stroked her gently, his fingertips executing a slow, deliberate circle.

Whimpering softly against the erotic sensation, she grasped his arm for support.

He kissed her tenderly while his fingers kept exploring. A warm, soft kiss of satisfaction.

Lust swamped her. She had to have him. Had to have him or she would surely die. She ran her tongue around his lips and he made a masculine noise of enjoyment.

He slipped her panties down then, edging them over her hips, below her thighs. When her panties fell to her ankles, she kicked them off and curled against him.

He sank slowly to his knees.

Uh-oh. What now?

She felt the touch of his lips against her upper thigh and pulled in a hissing breath as his mouth inched toward the place Katie most wanted him to touch with that quicksilver tongue.

Wanted it, but was she ready for it? Few had ever gone there. She put a hand to the back of his neck. "Wait, I…"

He lifted his head. "Don't be shy," he whispered, and then made a promise. "I won't hurt you."

His strong outer lips rested against her soft inner lips. Instant heat. Boiling, building. She was a teapot—hot and ready to let off steam. She had no idea she was capable of feeling such physical intensity.

He made a sound of hearty appreciation and clasped her tightly in his muscled arms, pressing her hips firmly against the wall. Pinning her. His prize.

Her hands were frantic, raking through his hair. She was desperate. Raw. Hungry need personified. Taking lust, turning it into trust.

Foolish, perhaps, but here she was.

She accepted what he gave her. She didn't ask for more. There was no reason. She did not require it. He conferred upon her everything she desired.

No one had ever touched her in the way Richard was touching her. Inside. Deep inside. He found all her secrets, exploited them to full advantage.

It felt so good it almost hurt. This free-falling pleasure and pain.

Lost. She was afloat in the sweep of his tongue, the moist heat of his mouth. The tension was impossible. His tongue teased and pleased. Taunted and tamed.

She wanted to cup his head in the back of her hands, drop to her knees and face him in the darkness.

But she was afraid. Afraid to learn too much. Afraid to ruin the fantasy. Afraid of being caught in a whirlwind of chaos from which she might never recover.

His head was buried between her legs, his tongue stroking her hooded femininity. She savored the wild ride. This encounter was special. Something she'd remember to the end of her days. She did not want reality to intrude.

He teased her clit, circling slowly at first, and then faster and firmer, pulling her toward a beautiful climax. But he wasn't going to let it be that easy. He eased off on the pressure, slowed down. And then he took her up again. Up and down in a tumult of sensation until she thought she'd go mad with need.

"I want to feel you inside me," she murmured. "I have to...*feel* you. Now."

He pulled back, rose to his feet. She heard him rustling. What was he doing? She was so wet and hot and achy. She needed him. Now, now, now.

"Do you have a condom?" she whispered.

"Got it covered," he said.

There was a slight tearing sound of a small package being opened.

She touched him down there, through the opening in his leather pants. Her hand closing around his steely shaft, and she heard his low groan of pleasure.

He was so hard. So big.

"Hurry," she insisted, growing suddenly scared against a nameless sense of dread crowding inside her chest. "Hurry, hurry, hurry."

"Wrap your legs around my waist," he said, pushing her shoulders against the wall, "and grab the clothing rods."

Heart pounding, she did as he asked. One hand wrapped around the hanging rod on the right, the other on the left, her legs serpentined around his hard waist. She could feel the tip of his penis throbbing against her bare buttocks.

She felt like an acrobat, a trapeze artist. It added to the excitement.

Carefully, he entered her warm wet center. She could feel the material of his pants rubbing against her thighs as he moved. Katie reflectively closed her eyes, gasping in reverence.

What an incredible sensation.

She was entranced, filled up by him. She relished the wonder of his body, the excitement of her fantasy, of the life force pulsing through him and into her and back again.

He pushed into the hilt.

And then he began a slow, meticulous thrusting.

Swept away, she matched his tempo, arching her back, pushing against him, using the hanging rods as a fulcrum, increasing the tension. The rhythm between them was quite extraordinary. They were so in tune with each other.

He thrust, she parried.

It was almost mystical.

This slow, sweet journey. The intensity rising and swelling, dropping and climbing.

"More," she gasped, barely hanging on to her French accent. "I've got to have more."

"Greedy," he accused.

Yes, yes, she was greedy and not the least bit remorseful.

Biting need flowed through her body. She needed this intimacy, needed him. Her legs were wrapped around his waist and she held him tightly.

The orgasm rose in her, in a hot, loud knot. She let go of the hanging rod so she could stuff her right fist against her mouth to hold back her cries of ecstasy.

He gave one last thrust and his body twitched with the power of his own climax. The sound of his breathing was rough against her ears.

And just after his release, she came as she'd never come before. Wave upon wave. An entire ocean crashing through her.

He held her as she shuddered in his arms. Then, after they'd recovered, he dressed her in the dark, tenderly slipping on her stockings and her shoes. When he was finished he pulled her to his chest and kissed her softly one last time.

"Oh, Richard." She breathed. "You were magnificent, as I knew you would be."

He made a startled noise and stepped away from her.

"What's wrong?" Katie felt his alarm. Hurriedly, she pulled the mask that had gotten pushed up on top of her head back down over her face and quickly adjusted her wig.

"Richard?"

He did not answer, but the coats mumbled as he brushed past them in his effort to get out of the closet and away from her.

Katie fumbled on the wall for the light switch and found it just as he opened the door.

The closet was bathed in light.

Their eyes met.

The pirate captain raised his palms. Katie found herself staring at the barbed-wire tattoo encircling his left wrist. Alarm shot through her, but her brain was still not processing what her eyes were telling her.

This man was not Richard Hancock.

This man was Liam James.

With dawning horror, Katie gasped and slapped a hand over her mouth. She'd just had sex with her sister's boyfriend!

STUNNED, Liam could only stare as the woman in the French-maid costume almost knocked him down getting past him. In the stark glare of the closet light bulb, he saw her auburn wig was knocked askew, blond curls were peeking out around it.

"Wait," he called.

She tossed him one last panic-stricken look over her shoulder. Even with the mask covering most of her face, she seemed oddly familiar. Did he know her?

He shook his head to clear it. Who?

Brooke. She reminded him of Brooke Winfield.

The synapses in his brain fired rapidly as alarming thoughts crowded in. Had Brooke dressed up in the French-maid costume to seduce him at the party? But Brooke had brown hair and she was taller than this woman.

And then it dawned on him and he recognized where he'd seen that saucy little walk before.

She was Katie Winfield. Brooke's baby sister.

Shoving a hand through his hair, Liam groaned aloud.

He had to go after her, had to explain himself. Had to *justify* what he'd done. Had to make sense of what they'd done together.

Liam took off after her, but she'd already disappeared in the crowd. People were staring at him, pointing and tittering. Agitated, he glanced down and saw that his bare chest was exposed from where Katie had ripped the buttons off his shirt and that his pants were unzipped.

Frantically, he tugged up his zipper as he ran. He was desperate to talk to her before she got away. But by the time he reached the front door, she'd already fled to the parking lot.

"Katie!" he yelled as he stumbled down the stairs and out onto the asphalt road, just as her red BMW convertible sped past him.

All he saw were her taillights disappearing into the darkness, leaving him feeling like the world's biggest jerk.

4

KATIE SPENT the remainder of the weekend holed up in her condo. She sprawled out on the couch, eating handfuls of caramel popcorn, guzzling hot chocolate and immersing herself in a romance-classics movie marathon. When Katie was a kid and feeling down in the dumps, her mother would get out the popcorn, the cocoa and the old movies to pick up her daughter's flagging spirits.

Normally the self-indulgent trick pulled Katie right out of the doldrums. This time, however, it hadn't worked. For one thing, it reminded her of Daisy and that made her sad. For another, watching lovers repeatedly meet, mingle, mate and marry hammered home what she already knew—sisters don't stab sisters in the back by sleeping with their boyfriends.

She would never be able to look Brooke in the eye again.

Cut yourself some slack. You didn't do it on purpose.

No, Katie might not have done it on purpose, but once again, she hadn't looked before she leaped. Witness the result of her recklessness.

She was so ashamed.

Brooke doesn't have to know. No one has to know.

Except Liam knew.

Maybe not, she hoped. Maybe he hadn't recognized her with the costume and the mask. She prayed it was so. But here was the terrible truth: sex with Liam was the best sex she'd ever had, and she wanted to do it again and again and again.

It wasn't him, she tried to convince herself. It was the masquerade, the semipublic location, the forbidden thrill of it all.

Oh God, she'd made such a mess of things.

By Monday evening, she was so sick of her own company she picked up the phone and called Tanisha.

"How was your weekend," she asked her best friend.

"Great," Tanisha purred like a satisfied kitten. "Dwayne and I spent the entire weekend in bed. In fact, he just left. How was your weekend?"

"Sucky."

Tanisha hissed in her breath. "Things didn't go so well with Richard?"

"I wasn't with Richard," Katie mumbled.

"Oh?"

"I had sex with my sister's boyfriend," she blurted.

"What?"

"I didn't mean to," Katie wailed. "I thought he was Richard. He was wearing a pirate costume. It was an honest mistake but now I feel so—"

"Hold the phone, girlfriend. I'll be right over."

An hour later, Tanisha showed up on her doorstep, a bag of takeout from the Chinese restaurant down the block clutched in her hand and a half gallon of chocolate-chip-cookie-dough ice cream in the other.

"This sounded like the kind of emergency best soothed by food," she explained, and breezed into the condo. "Besides, I'm starving. Dwayne and I must have burned up a thousand calories."

"Braggart," Katie accused.

"Don't pretend you wouldn't be doing some bragging of your own if the shoe was on the other foot." Tanisha dished up sweet-and-sour chicken and several kinds of dim sum on two paper plates. She passed one of the plates to Katie and handed her a set of chopsticks.

The delicious smell teased Katie's nose and she realized she hadn't eaten anything but caramel popcorn all weekend long. They sat at the wrought iron bistro table in the breakfast nook.

"Give me all the details," Tanisha said. "Don't leave anything out."

Cringing, Katie told her everything.

"Look," Tanisha said when she'd finished, "it was a case of mistaken identity. No one can fault you for that. If anything, he's the one who should be ashamed for sneaking off with someone else when he's dating your sister."

"That's true." She perked up. "But it doesn't change the fact that I betrayed Brooke."

"You didn't do it on purpose. How serious is Brooke and this guy, anyway? And what's his name?"

"Liam James."

Tanisha's eyes widened. "The real-estate mogul who was nominated Boston's most eligible bachelor by *Young Bostonian?*"

"That'd be the one."

"All I gotta say is, girl, when you screw up, you do it in *style*."

Katie groaned and sank her head in her hands. "I don't know what to do."

"Don't do anything." Tanisha shrugged. "Forget all about it."

"I can't."

Tanisha studied her for a moment. "This is really eating you up inside, isn't it?"

Katie nodded miserably.

"Your guilt only underscores what I was trying to tell you on Friday."

"Which is?"

"You're into self-sabotage."

"You're probably right," Katie said glumly, poking at her dim sum with a chopstick. Of all the dumb things she'd done in her life, this had to be one of the dumbest.

"There's a cure, you know."

Katie looked up from her plate. "And that is?"

"Give up casual sex."

Katie arched an eyebrow. "This coming from the queen of casual sex."

"Not anymore," Tanisha said.

"Oh?" Katie straightened.

Tanisha giggled girlishly, which was a surprise because she was not the giggly type. She pulled a key from her pocket. "Dwayne gave me a key to his place and I gave him one to mine."

"Seriously?"

"I think my wild partying days are behind me."

"That's great." Katie got up to give her friend a hug.

"Thanks," Tanisha beamed. "I feel so happy."

"I'm happy for you."

"I wish you could find someone. When was the last time you had a serious boyfriend?"

Katie gulped. She'd never had a serious boyfriend. She'd been having too much fun playing the field. "I'm not really ready for a serious relationship. I just want to stop making stupid mistakes."

"Then turn over a new leaf and empower yourself."

"I thought I was empowered."

"If you were empowered, then you wouldn't be feeling miserable over it."

Katie blew out her breath. "Okay, so how do I empower myself?"

"Stop basing your decisions on an if-it-feels-good-do-it philosophy. Think about the consequences of your actions," Tanisha instructed.

"Can you bottom-line it for me?"

"When it comes to sex, you're going to have to go cold turkey."

LIAM SPENT the weekend working. Or at least trying to work.

Hell, who was he kidding? He hadn't gotten a lick of work done. He'd spent Saturday and Sunday at the office staring at the contracts on his desk and all he could see was Katie Winfield decked out in that devastating French-maid outfit.

He had taken his anger at Finn Delancy out on her, and he had no idea how to make amends.

Maybe you shouldn't make amends. Maybe you

should leave well enough alone. She's obviously embarrassed that she mistook you for this Richard dude, or she wouldn't have run off. Let it go.

But Monday afternoon, when he still hadn't been able to concentrate, he was starting to get concerned. He'd never been stymied like this. He didn't like it. To clear his head, he went for a jog in the park, but it didn't help.

Finally, not knowing what else to do, he telephoned Tony.

"Red Sox are playing tonight," Liam said. "Wanna go?"

"Just you and me?"

"Yes. Unless Jess wants to come."

"She's over at her sister's helping her redecorate her living room."

"So we're on?"

"I don't believe it. You? Taking time out for a ball game with your best buddy?"

"We've got season tickets, no sense in wasting them."

"But we haven't gone to a game without a business client tagging along since...well, never."

"We went in college."

"No, we didn't."

"Really? I could have sworn we did."

"Didn't happen."

"Well, I guess it's time we rectified my oversight. Meet you at the ticket counter. They throw out the first pitch at seven."

Tony was lounging at the front gate when Liam arrived at Fenway Park.

"You gonna tell me what this is really about?" Tony asked as they made their way to their seats juggling beers and hot dogs.

"What? I want to watch a few innings with my best friend."

"You sure there's not something you want to tell me?"

"No."

"Okay, I'll take your word for it. But if there was something, you'd tell me, right?"

"You'd be the first to know."

"I doubt it," Tony mumbled.

"What's that?"

"You keep everything bottled up, buttoned down. You don't talk to anybody about anything except work." Tony waved at hand at Liam's starched shirt. "I mean, have you ever in your life, just once, let yourself go?"

"No," he said, but then he thought, *French maid in a closet.*

"What are you so afraid of?" Tony asked.

"Who says I'm afraid of anything?"

"Everybody's afraid of something. I'm trying to figure out why you push yourself so hard?"

It sounded like a dumb question to him. How could he not push himself hard? He had a lot to prove. "Money," he said.

"Don't give me that. You have enough money to last you a lifetime."

What was he afraid of? Failure? Falling in love? He gulped back a swallow of beer. "Okay," Liam admitted after a long moment, "it's about a woman."

Tony sat up straighter. "Brooke?"

"No. Her sister, Katie."

"I'm listening."

Liam glanced over his shoulder to see how close the nearest fan was sitting and lowered his voice. "I hooked up with her at the masquerade party."

"Hooked up as in—"

"Yeah."

Tony whistled and slugged him lightly on the upper arm. "You dog. Who knew you had it in you?"

Liam glowered. "What's that supposed to mean?"

Balancing his hot dog on one knee, Tony held up a palm. "Nothing, dude. Settle."

Agitation had him shifting in his seat. "The deal is, I can't get her out of my head."

"That's not a bad thing."

"Of course it is. I can't concentrate on work."

"You've never really felt this way about a woman before?"

"No."

"How many girlfriends have you had?"

Liam shrugged. "I don't know. Six, seven. But none of them ever messed with my head like this." Other than Arianna, and that was a whole different kind of head game.

"That's because—since I've known you anyway— you've always picked career-driven women who complemented your lifestyle. You've never been out with one who made your question your priorities."

"Exactly."

"Maybe that's the problem."

"I'm not following you."

"Katie Winfield, this woman you hooked up with at the party, she's different."

Liam nodded.

"Totally not right for you. Impulsive, I'm guessing. Adventuresome."

"Yes, yes." Impatiently, he tapped his fingertips on the back of the seat in front of him. "What's your point?"

"For the first time in your life you've found a woman who makes you feel totally alive."

He wanted to deny it, but it was true.

"Compared to her," Tony went on, "work seems dull and pointless."

"What's wrong with me?"

"Got bad news for you, buddy boy." Tony grinned. "There's only one way to beat this thing."

"How's that?"

"Embrace it."

Liam didn't like the direction this conversation was headed. "What do you mean, embrace it?"

"You've been working nonstop since you were what? Sixteen?"

"Yeah."

"And all this time, you've been keeping your emotions in check."

"What's your point?"

"It was bound to happen."

Frustration had him fisting his hand around his beer. "What was bound to happen?"

"You gotta have a little fun at some point. Kick up your heels. Let your libido run wild."

"You think so? You think if I embrace this feeling and go with it, have a good time with this woman, it will eventually pass and then I can get back to work?"

"That's what I'm saying."

Hmm. It was a thought.

"So what does Katie Winfield do for a living?" Tony asked.

"She's a graphic designer at a small advertising agency."

"There you go. It's perfect." Tony dabbed mustard off his chin with a green napkin.

"There I go where?"

"Hire her advertising agency to do some work for us. Those downtown warehouses you've renovated into condos are opening soon. Throw the ad campaign her way."

"And then what?"

"Seduce her. Have a good time if she's game. Besides, it's way past time you sowed a few wild oats."

"You think that would work?"

"Worth a shot. Here we go boys!" Tony jumped to his feet and almost spilled his beer. "Home run Red Sox!"

COLD TURKEY?

Easy for Tanisha to say. She had a key to her boyfriend's place. Katie had to admit she was jealous.

And lonely.

Maybe Tanisha was right. Maybe it was time for her to turn over a new leaf.

Bright and early Tuesday morning, Max stuck his head into the office she shared with Tanisha. "Excuse me, ladies. We have a new client. Meeting in the conference room at ten."

"Should we put together a preliminary pitch before the meeting?" Katie asked. "Who's the client?"

"He's only here to get preliminary bids. But bring your A game. This fish is a big one."

An hour later, the creative team assembled in the conference room, buzzing with speculation about this new high-profile project. Katie was still preoccupied with what had happened at the Ladies League ball and she wasn't paying much attention.

That is until the door to the conference room opened and Max walked in, followed by their new client.

At the sight of him, Katie's heart stumbled drunkenly against her rib cage. She couldn't believe what she was seeing.

Liam James, wrist tattoo and all, came striding into the room as if he owned it.

The memory of their rendezvous in the cloak closet came rushing back in gloriously shameful detail. The hot kisses, the frantic shedding of clothes, the quick, powerful thrusts in the inky blackness.

She hiccoughed.

Did he recognize her? Katie kept her head down as she slipped into a leather swivel chair at the far end of the conference table and prayed that he did not.

Max went around the room, introducing him to everyone on the team. When Liam's eyes lighted on Katie, a bone-clutching chill shot through her, immediately followed by a gush of thrilling heat.

Oh, this was bad.

"Katie," he said, his voice oozing charm. "It's nice to see you again."

What did he mean by that remark?

He shook her hand and her gaze fixed on the now familiar barbed-wire tattoo encircling his wrist. A quick pulse of energy surged between them.

Lightning in a jar.

She jerked her hand back from the contact. His hazel eyes darkened and a slight but suggestive smile tipped his lips.

He knew!

"Hi," she said because that was all she could manage to squeeze past her constricted throat.

Play it cool and act as if Friday night never happened. You're going cold turkey.

"You two know each other?" Max arched an eyebrow.

"He's dating my sister," Katie explained.

"I'm not." Liam's eyes never left her face. "Brooke and I are just friends."

"Really?"

"Really." He smiled at her.

Relief washed over Katie, along with a surge of hope and a heightened sense of excitement. *Settle down.*

Liam turned to Max. "Actually, Katie's the reason I'm here."

"Really?" Max said archly.

"I've seen the graphic designs she did for the new campaign for Worthington's Department Store. She's a very talented artist. You scored big when you hired her."

Liam's compliment brought a flush of pride to

Katie's cheeks. Brooke worked for Worthington's and she must have been the one to show Liam her design.

Max looked at Katie as if seeing her for the first time. "She's not bad. A bit raw, but maybe she could become great with time and dedication."

Coming from Max, that was a magnanimous admission.

Liam, broad shouldered and lean hipped, pulled out the chair beside Katie and sat down. Her heart thumped.

My legs have been wrapped around those hips, she thought.

The large conference room suddenly seemed claustrophobically small sitting this close to him, his crisp, masculine scent wafting over her. He smelled startlingly wonderful—like minty toothpaste mingled with rainy autumn days and…sweet, sweet sin.

Max took a seat, as well, steepled his fingertips and leaned forward. "So tell us about your new project, Mr. James."

"Well," Liam said, his gaze lingering on Katie so long she was certain he must have guessed her secret identity. She wanted to look away, but she simply could not. "It's all about sex."

"SEX?" Katie whispered.

Sex?

What in the devil had made him say that?

Katie Winfield, that's who.

Liam hadn't failed to notice the sweet curve of her ass as she'd gracefully eased it down into the plush leather chair. His palms itched to knead her sweet, firm flesh sheathed so provocatively by the silky material of her skirt. The strength of his need was shocking.

She was staring him straight in the eyes, not intimidated in the least by his frank appraisal.

Courageous. He liked that.

His gaze fell to her full, feminine mouth and hung there. God, she had gorgeous lips. It felt as if the conference room were empty and the world had narrowed to just the two of them. Staring into her eyes, Liam recognized the same out-of-control sensation that had gripped him at the masquerade party.

"Sex," he repeated, as if that's what he'd intended on saying all along. "I'm renovating downtown warehouses into condos and I want an ad campaign that appeals to hip, young, well-to-do urbanites."

"And sex sells," Katie said.

"Exactly."

"We can do that," Max Kruger interjected.

"But," Liam spoke, never taking his gaze off Katie, "I want Katie in as the art director."

"Katie?" Max sounded nonplussed.

"Me?" Katie squeaked.

"You."

"Katie's never served as art director on a campaign," Max said.

"First time for everything," Liam replied.

"Max is right," Katie said. "I'd be out of my league."

Liam shrugged and started to get up. "All right, if you don't think you can handle success."

"Excuse me." Katie's eyes sparked.

Had he made her mad?

"Could I speak to you out in the hallway for a moment?"

"Me?" He arched an eyebrow.

"You," she said curtly.

"Why, sure." Liam couldn't stop the grin this time. "Max, do you mind?"

"It's your dime." Max waved a hand.

Katie marched out into the hallway. Liam followed leisurely, enjoying the view below her flouncing skirt hem. Damn, but the woman had a gorgeous pair of legs.

She pulled the door closed tight after him, sank her hands on her hips and spun to face him. "What in the hell are you trying to pull?"

"Excuse me?"

"Don't play innocent with me. I know what you're up to."

"You do?"

"Yes, and stop smiling at me."

"You don't like being smiled at?"

"Not by you."

"What's wrong with me?" He was enjoying teasing her.

"You…you dressed up like Captain Jack and took advantage of my case of mistaken identity."

"Hey, now—" he raised a finger "—you were the one who pulled me into the closet."

"So why did you come here today?" She folded her arms protectively over her chest.

"To get an ad campaign rolling for my new condos."

"Liar."

"Okay," he admitted, "that wasn't the only reason I

chose Sharper Designs. I wanted to see you again, Katie, and apologize for what happened in the closet."

"There's nothing to apologize for. It happened. It's over, and now that I know you're not Brooke's boyfriend, well, I don't even have to feel guilty about it anymore, now do I?"

Liam angled his head and studied her face for a long moment. In spite of her words, she was still feeling guilty. "You made quite an impression on me."

"Let's get something straight," she said. "You're hiring my talents as a graphic designer, nothing more. As far as I'm concerned, Friday never happened. Got it?"

"Yes, ma'am."

"You're still doing it," she said.

"Doing what?"

"Smiling at me. Stop smiling at me."

"What's wrong with smiling?"

"Because you look adorable when you smile."

"I know," he said, his grin widening. "I'm trying to be irresistible."

"It's not working," she muttered. "You're resistible."

"You are such a bad liar."

Her earlobes turned pink. She ducked her head, but then peeked up at him from underneath those long eyelashes. His heart slammed when he spied the hint of vulnerability in those blue depths. Her eyes narrowed the world to only him.

Liam felt special.

In a nervous gesture, she slipped her fingers through her hair, and tucked a sleek blond strand behind one perfectly shaped ear. Her breasts rose and fell beneath the

V-neck of her crisp white blouse, and he spied the sexy blush of a pink bra underneath the white top.

Oh, yeah, she knew how to get to a man.

She spun another strand of golden hair around an index finger in a graceful motion. Her fingernails, he noted, were painted a soft high-society color of pale rose. She wore a single gold chain around her neck and her earrings were plain gold studs. But everything she had on was of the highest quality. It was the understated attire of a true blue blood.

She was contradictory. There were her classically tailored work clothes, and then there was the French-maid persona she let loose in closets. He liked the paradox.

His gaze hung on her lips. Rich, ripe, painted the color of summer strawberries. He caught his breath and waited.

For what, he didn't know.

Katie flicked out her tongue and touched the tip of it to the glistening gloss of her upper lip. Slowly, she traced around the moist pink edges of her mouth with the cool certainty of a woman who knew exactly the effect she had on a man.

The overhead florescent hallway lighting slanted a shaft of illumination across her face. He looked down at her and was surprised to see a glimpse of sadness in her eyes. Tender feelings rose up in him. Feelings he'd never felt before and didn't understand.

As they stared into each other's eyes, the air leaked from their lungs in a simultaneous exhale.

Liam knew he was a goner. His gaze beaded on her

lips. Lips he yearned to kiss again. He leaned forward, resting his arm on the wall above her head. Not thinking, just wanting.

Katie didn't pull away. She was so near he could feel the heat of her skin. If they weren't standing in the corridor of Sharper Designs, he would have kissed her.

They stared at one another with an astonishing mix of surprise, delight and stark sexual heat. He had to have her. Tony was right. The only way he was ever going to get Katie out of his system was to embrace his desires and find a way to charm this bedazzling woman into his bed.

"I'm coming back on Friday. Around one o'clock," he said. "That gives you three days to come up with an art design for my condos. Do you think you can handle it?"

She lifted her chin. "I can handle it."

"Oh, and there's one other thing."

"What's that?" she asked.

"I'm expecting to have my socks blown off."

5

"ARE YOU SURE it has to be cold turkey?" Katie asked Tanisha after Liam had left Sharper Designs and they were in their office again. "Can't I sort of taper off impulsive sex?"

"Absolutely not. It's like when you've convinced yourself you're only going to have one Oreo cookie and you end up scarfing down the whole box."

"You are a tough taskmaster," Katie grumbled.

"It's for your own good," Tanisha said sagely. "Builds character."

"Sure, I'd like to see how good you'd be at giving up sex."

"I'm not the one who was caught doing the deed with the wrong man at a masquerade party."

"Touché." Yes, while initially Liam might have been the wrong man, Katie found herself wondering if fate, in its roundabout way, might have actually dealt her the *right* man.

She thought of how he'd stared at her when she'd called him out into the hallway for their private chat. How very close his lips had been to hers. She felt hot and bothered all over. But before she had time to fully ride that train of thought Max marched into the office.

"Winfield," he barked.

"Yes, sir?"

"I don't have to tell you what landing the James account means to this firm."

"No, sir."

"And if making you art director is what it takes to seal the deal, then of course, I'm agreeing to it."

"Uh-huh."

"But I'm not happy about this development. I don't know what you've got going on with Liam—"

"Sir, let me assure you, there's nothing going on," Katie said.

Max snorted. "Please, I saw the way the man was staring at you. If nothing is going on yet, then he's looking to start something up."

Katie's face heated. Was their attraction that obvious? "Nothing's going on," she reiterated. Hadn't she just turned over a new leaf?

Max impatiently waved away her denial. "Here it is. I don't know what's happening with you two and I really don't care. All I care is that you pull off this campaign to his satisfaction. Personally, I don't think you're ready for the art-director position. You're too young, too unmotivated."

She opened her mouth to protest, but Max cut her off. "I'm giving you the benefit of the doubt. Do well with this project and the promotion will be permanent. But if you screw this up, you're out on your can. Got it?"

"Got it." She resisted the urge to salute.

"As long as we're clear on this. Now, get to work." Max turned and stalked out of the office.

Katie slumped down in her chair. Talk about pressure.

She only had three measly days to come up with a design plan that would blow Liam's socks off. If she wanted to keep her job, she had to make sure their attraction stayed firmly under control.

How to accomplish both goals?

She spent the remainder of the workday pondering the question. On the way to her car that evening, she passed by the pet shop and noticed that the cocker spaniel was still in the window. The minute the pup spied her, he went up on his hind legs, pushing his front paws up against the glass, tail wagging madly.

"Hey, boy." She greeted him.

The pup barked.

Katie started to back up.

He barked louder.

Katie's heart melted. She cupped her hands around her eyes, pressed her face to the glass. The lights were on inside and she saw customers moving around. The store was still open.

The quaint silver bell over the door tinkled welcomingly as Katie stepped inside. The woman behind the counter greeted her with a New Englander's slow, syllabled "Hey-ya."

"Hello." Katie smiled at the woman, but her eyes were on the puppy. She leaned over the barrier keeping the cocker penned in the window and tickled her fingers over his soft fur. The puppy licked Katie's hand with his warm, wet tongue.

Katie giggled.

It would be so easy to fall in love with him.

Like there's any room in your life for a pet. You, who've killed every houseplant you've ever owned.

Yes, but she was doing things differently now. No more late-night partying. No more random hookups. No more impromptu weekend trips out of town. There would be room in her new lifestyle for a puppy.

It was a nice thought.

Better make sure the changes stick before you rush headlong into buying a dog.

Yes, just because she was giving up men didn't mean she could use a puppy as a substitute. Sighing wistfully, she left the pet shop.

Twenty minutes later, she walked through the door of her condo, the daily mail tucked under her arm. She kicked off her stilettos in the foyer, tossed her sweater over the back of a kitchen chair, then made a beeline for the refrigerator and the leftover dim sum takeout Tanisha had brought over the night before.

She heated the food in the microwave and ate standing over the sink as she leafed through the stack of mail. Catalog, catalog, bill, circular. She tossed those aside, but stopped when she came to a jazzy pink envelope with her name embossed with gold foil calligraphy.

Hmm, what was this?

It looked interesting. She glanced at the return address, saw it was from a nightclub called Chassys. Frowning, Katie tore into the envelope, trying to remember if she'd ever been to this bar.

Dear Ms. Winfield,
You are invited to join Martinis and Bikinis. We

are a social club offering group encouragement and support for women seeking personal growth and empowerment through pushing themselves outside their comfort zone.

You are exactly the kind of member we're looking for.

Smart, educated, influential. If you're interested in joining our group, we meet the first Thursday of every month at Chassys nightclub. Please find driving directions enclosed. We're looking forward to meeting you.

Sincerely,

Lindsay Beckham

President, Martinis and Bikinis

How timely. It was as if this Lindsay Beckham person had read her mind. Empowerment and personal growth. That was exactly what she needed right now.

And the Martinis and Bikinis' next meeting was this Thursday.

What did she have to lose? She might as well go. Who knew? This group might be the thing she needed to stick with her new plan to tread the straight and narrow.

WHEN THURSDAY evening rolled around, Katie dressed in black slacks, a blue-and-white angora sweater, black boots and modest gold jewelry. Following the driving directions that accompanied the invitation, she ended up in an older neighborhood of South Boston, currently undergoing an economic resurgence.

Chassys was located at 431 Beaumont Street in an

older brick building next door to the Yarn Barn. Just a few buildings down from a brand-new Starbucks. Here, apartments were located over most of the shops, restaurants and nightclubs. After circling the crowded block a couple of times, she found a parking spot on a side street and walked back to the bar. Her boots clacked with a clear, determined sound against the uneven sidewalk.

This is it. The fresh start to my new life. Viva female empowerment.

It was a high-traffic area. This time of the evening, there were lots of couples and groups of young singles milling about. The area was a far cry from the upscale establishments she normally frequented.

But when she pushed through the mahogany-paneled door, Katie stepped into a dazzling oasis. Chassys was unexpectedly classy. The furnishings were sleek, new and thoroughly modern.

The floor was constructed of a cherry hardwood, the bar and tabletops dark granite. The barstools were black leather with chrome trim. White Japanese lanterns hung from the ceiling, offering lots of subtle lighting. Chic, atmospheric music filtered in through a state-of-the art sound system, setting the mood with a rhythmic beat.

The bar was packed with a hip, lively crowd and Katie, who was usually right at home in nightclub hot spots, suddenly felt intimidated. Clutching the invitation in her hand, she inched her way through the crowd and headed for the bar.

"What can I get you?" asked the hunky, dark-haired bartender in black denim and a black T-shirt, who had to shout to be heard over the humming throng. Any other time, Katie might have been inclined to tease him. But she'd put aside her flirtatious ways.

"I'm here for a meeting," she shouted back and waved the invitation for him to see.

"Then you'll be wanting the Passion-tini."

"No—" she shook her head "—I got invited to join a group called Martinis and Bikinis."

"That's right." He nodded and flashed a white-toothed grin. "Chassys prepares a different Bikinitini every month. September is Passion-tini month. It's a sassy mixture of passion fruit, mint, fresh lime juice and citrus vodka. Addictive stuff."

"Hook me up."

He made the drink and slid it across the bar. She reached in her purse for a twenty, but he held up his palm. "Drinks are on the house for Martinis and Bikinis first timers."

"Really?" Ooh, she liked this club already. "Thanks."

"The group is meeting right through there." He jerked his thumb toward a curtain at the back of the room. "I think everyone's pretty much here."

Suddenly, she felt a little weak-kneed with nervousness. Katie took a long pull of the Passion-tini. It was delicious and powerful enough to bolster her determination to change her life.

Tentatively, she edged back the black silk curtain and stepped into a room with black upholstered banquettes on both sides and several small tables in the middle of the room.

There were about thirty women in attendance, each holding a Passion-tini and clustered in small groups, engaged in animated conversations. Apparently the official meeting had yet to begin.

Not knowing anyone, Katie felt out of place.

A tall elegant-looking blonde standing in the front of the room caught Katie's attention. Her hair was combed back off her forehead, revealing a stunning widow's peak. She had high, beautiful cheekbones that put her in mind of Meryl Streep. Her eyes were deep blue and she had a smile on her face, but it was easy to see she was a reserved woman who held her real emotions closely in check.

"Hiya," said a short, breathy-voiced woman with curly auburn hair, snapping brown eyes and apple-dumpling cheeks. She stuck her hand out. "You must be new. I'm Tanya."

One look in Tanya's eyes and she immediately felt welcome. "Nice to meet you, Tanya. I'm Katie."

"I just joined M&B a few months ago myself." Tanya giggled. "I kid you not. These ladies saved my life after a lousy divorce. Are you divorced? A lot of women join M&B after a divorce."

"Never married."

"Good for you. That's one way to avoid ending up with a louse." Tanya giggled again and that's when Katie realized the giggling was a dodge for her nervousness. Knowing Tanya was nervous, as well, soothed Katie's own trepidation.

"Who's that?" Katie nodded her head at the sleek blonde.

"Oh, that's Lindsay Beckham. She's the owner of Chassys and founder of our group. She's quite the businesswoman and so daring. She's an example for us all. She's helped empower so many women. Including my best pal, Kim."

"Which one is Kim?"

"She's not here tonight." Giggling, Tanya lowered her voice. "She's recovering from getting a boob job that was part of her Martini dare."

"Martini dare?"

"You'll see. It's the reason for the club. The group dares you to go beyond your comfort zone and then offers emotional support for you in the process."

"So let me get this straight. The group dared your friend Kim to get a boob job?"

Tanya shook her head. "No, they dared her to do something she'd always wanted to do, but had been too afraid to take the leap."

"So what have you dared?" Katie leaned down closer to whisper to Tanya and her gaze strayed to the woman's ample bosom.

Tanya caught the look, giggled and wiggled proudly. "These are all me. I haven't done a dare yet."

"How come?"

"Lindsay doesn't think I'm ready."

"Oh, so Lindsay gets to decide who takes a dare and when?"

"Uh-huh."

"Lindsay sounds like a bit of a control freak."

Tanya's eyes widened as she looked around Katie's shoulder. "Um, Katie…"

"She's standing right behind me, isn't she?"

Tanya just giggled.

Oh, gosh, when was she ever going to learn to keep her big trap shut? This certainly wasn't an auspicious start to her first Martinis and Bikinis meeting.

Cringing, Katie turned to face the woman and sheepishly wiggled her fingertips. "Hi, there."

"Lindsay Beckham, resident control freak." A bemused look was in the woman's eyes, but she wasn't smiling. Katie couldn't tell if she was pissed off or amused.

"Katie Winfield."

Lindsay studied her with an appraising look and she took so long in responding that Katie began to think it might be best if she just slunk out of there.

"I have an invitation." She held it up. "See?"

Lindsay looked past Katie. "You came alone?"

"Uh-huh."

"Well, it's nice to have you. Please take a seat. The meeting is about to start."

Tanya plopped down at an empty table and patted the seat next to her. Kate sat down beside her.

The program started with the women who'd completed their dares from the previous month regaling the rest of the audience with the details of their adventures. One woman had gone skydiving, and she rhapsodized about the experience. Another had dared to ask out her handsome new neighbor, only to discover to her disappointment that he was gay.

The group gave them a rousing round of applause and then Lindsay stepped up again. "And now, we've reached the part of the evening where two members of our group are chosen to pick a scroll from the sacred Box of Dares."

A ripple of excitement ran through the crowd as Lindsay made a big production of bringing out a heavy wooden box.

"As always, we recite the rules first." Lindsay pantomimed unrolling a parchment and held up the invisible rules in front of her. "The members chosen for the dare must be approved by a majority of the membership present. As you swore when you joined Martinis and Bikinis, once you agree to pick a dare, there's no backing out. Period. Even quitting the group will not exempt you from your most serious obligation." She looked out over the gathered women. "Hands up if you understand."

Everyone except Katie raised their hands. She was only visiting.

"Then by the completely nonimportant authority vested in me by the Martinis and Bikinis Organization, I announce that Sherry will take the first dare this month. Everyone agree?"

It was a unanimous vote.

Sherry, a thin but curvaceous blonde with short spiked hair and crimson lipstick, bounced up to the front of the room. Katie noticed her hand shook slightly as she drew out a scrolled piece of parchment wrapped with a red ribbon. These women took their dares seriously.

After untying the ribbon, Sherry rolled down the scroll and read her dare aloud. "Take a ride in an expensive Italian sports car, but do it completely in the nude."

The women hooted and catcalled and craned forward with interest. "Go, Sherry!" someone shouted.

Pfft, that sounded easy to Katie. She thought of the

Babes Gone Braless video she'd appeared in during spring break her sophomore year of college. Now that was a dare.

Remember, you've sworn off doing rash things. Maybe this group isn't for you if they encourage people to do rash things.

"Katie." Lindsay held up the box and shook it. "Your turn."

She splayed a hand to her chest. "Me?"

"Yes, you."

"But…but I'm new."

Lindsay looked around at the group. "Anyone opposed to Katie picking tonight?"

Katie was the only one who raised her hand.

"Majority rules." Lindsay wagged the box. "You're up."

"I'm not even an official member," Katie protested.

"You can join tonight."

Katie shook her head. "I'm not sure I'm ready to make that commitment."

"What's the matter? Are you too afraid to empower your life?" Lindsay challenged.

Katie narrowed her eyes. She knew what this was about. Lindsay was getting even with her for that control-freak comment by making her choose a dare on her very first night.

Not one to back down from a challenge, Katie shot to her feet. For a split second, a wave of panic washed over her. Here she was again, jumping headlong into something without considering the consequences. But she wasn't about to let Lindsay see her hesitate.

With a toss of her head, she marched to the front of the room, stuck her hand in the box and drew her first dare.

She slipped the red velvet ribbon from the crisp parchment scroll, unrolled it and read out loud to the room. "You have drawn a three-part dare. Each of your dares is to be completed within one week's time. The second and third dares will be mailed to reach you by the Thursday of each week. For this week, your dare is to make love to the man of your dreams in a forbidden place."

Stunned, Katie turned to gape at Lindsay. It was as if the dare had been tailor-made for her. Correction. Tailor-made for the old Katie. The one who used to do foolish things like make love to strangers in closets.

"Ball's in your court, Katie." Lindsay smirked. "Are you all talk? Or do you dare?"

ANTICIPATION.

A heightened sense of expectation had been nipping at his heels for three days. Liam was so stoked about seeing Katie again that he pulled into the secure parking lot three blocks down from Sharper Designs fifteen minutes ahead of their scheduled Friday meeting.

All week long, he'd kept thinking about Tony's advice.

Seduce Katie Winfield. Have a good time. Sow a few wild oats.

His body tensed with the thought of her. His mouth filled with the remembered taste of her sweet lips as he hopped out of his Lamborghini, briefcase in tow and headed for Sharper Designs.

And then, as if he'd conjured her from thin air, Liam

spied Katie standing on the sidewalk, peering into the window of a pet store.

Irresistibly, his eyes were drawn to her. Her sleek blond Boston Brahmin hair was capped off by a bright red beret. She looked incredibly jaunty as she raised a lithe hand, doffed the beret and lightly combed her fingers through her tousled tresses before putting it back on again.

She wore a soft fuzzy sweater the same color as the beret. He had no doubt it was made from the finest cashmere. The hem of her swingy black skirt molded to her slim thighs when she moved, fluid as water. Just watching her caused his muscles to tighten.

She seemed to encapsulate all the things he longed for, but feared he could never have. Good breeding, perfect manners, high-born status. A genuine sense of fun.

Did she have any idea how impossibly beautiful she was, with that silky smooth skin, long, swanlike neck and the cutest little overbite. Did she have a clue as to how many men would give their right arm to be with her?

"Fancy meeting you here," he said as he approached, but then felt like a total idiot for saying something so stupid and clichéd. Smooth move from the guy dubbed Boston's most eligible bachelor of the year by *Young Bostonian* magazine.

She turned and the minute she saw him, her face lit up, warming him from the inside out. "Liam."

Their gazes met and he saw such a melancholic expression come into her eyes that it made him pause.

What was she so sad about?

His gaze drifted to the pet-shop window. There was

a cocker-spaniel puppy in the window, paws pressed against the glass, eyeing Katie with total puppy love. A feeling he understood well.

"Friend of yours?" He smiled.

"I drop by to see him every day on my lunch hour. Sometimes I even go in to pet him. Honestly, I can't understand why he hasn't been adopted. Isn't he the most adorable thing?"

"Yes, he is," Liam said, but he was looking at her, not the puppy. "Why don't *you* buy him?"

"Me? Oh, no." She shook her head. "I can't even keep goldfish alive."

"Says who?"

"Everyone in my family." She chuckled. "Just ask them."

"I'm not asking everyone in your family," he said. "I'm asking you."

Katie shrugged. "My apartment doesn't allow pets."

"Oh, is that it?"

"Yeah, that's it."

His gaze caught lazily on her lips. "Would you like to take him for a walk?"

"We've got a meeting in ten minutes."

"I'm the client. I can delay the meeting if I want to. Would you like to take the puppy for a walk?"

"We could do that?"

He shrugged. "When you're Boston's most eligible bachelor…"

"You can do anything," she finished for him, and grinned.

"You've got it."

"But what's Max going to say?"

"Let me take care of Max." Liam pulled out his cell phone and gave Max Kruger a call to tell him he was commandeering his employee and pushing the meeting back for half an hour. "We're all set."

Five minutes later, Liam and Katie left the pet shop with the exuberant puppy, headed for the nearby park. The sun was warm, the breeze cool and the smell of autumn crisp and fresh. The puppy tugged hard on the leash, happy to be out of the window and exploring the world.

"Did you ever have a dog when you were growing up?" Liam asked.

"Once, but I wasn't allowed to keep him. Brooke turned out to be allergic. You?"

He shook his head. "We couldn't afford the food and vet bills."

"Poor us. We've been so deprived." She laughed; a soft melodic sound that lit him up inside.

You can say that again.

"Look at the way his hair flows, so soft and silky."

"I'm looking," he said, but his eyes weren't on the cocker spaniel.

"He's so proud and proper, the way he holds his head up and prances." Katie tilted her own head. "I wonder if he has a pedigree."

"Why do you think I had to put down a three-hundred-dollar deposit just to take him for a walk?"

She graced him ˙ ˙ ˙ a beatific smile. "Thank you for that."

"You could change apartments, you know?"

"What?"

"If you wanted to buy him, that is. You could always move."

"It'd be a big commitment," she hedged.

"Yeah," he said.

"I'm not ready to tackle such a long-term obligation."

"If you were ready, what would you name him?"

"Something befitting his nobility. Duke, perhaps. That's what I named the puppy that was mine for a weekend."

"It suits him." He nodded.

"Oh, look," she said, "an ice-cream vendor. Want some?"

Without waiting for an answer, she and Duke took off toward the ice-cream vendor pushing his cart through the park. Liam tagged along, enjoying her enthusiasm.

She bought an orange push-up. Liam hadn't seen one since he was a kid. It was orange-flavored ice cream on a stick wrapped up in a cardboard container festooned with cartoon characters. You were supposed to push up the ice cream as you ate it. The theory was the cardboard kept sticky confections off messy children.

"Mmm, wanna bite?" She pushed up the orange ice cream and offered it to him.

"No, that's okay. You go ahead."

"Come on. It's great." She waggled it under his nose. "I dare you."

He smiled, shook his head.

"What? Are you afraid I'll give you girl cooties?"

Cooties. Something else he hadn't heard since childhood.

"I'm not afraid of girl cooties."

"Prove it," she goaded.

She had no idea of the craving ripping and clawing through him as he looked at her lips, dotted with a spot of ice cream, or she wouldn't tempt him so glibly. If she had the slightest idea about the appetites he kept tightly leashed, the hunger that even now, in this park, in the bright light of the noonday sun, stressed every atom of his self-control, she would run for her life.

Liam didn't want to eat ice cream. He wanted to eat her.

"Come on," she cajoled.

Impulsively, he bit off a bite of her push-up. She was right. It tasted delicious.

He thought he might scare her with his abrupt about-face, the slippage of his control. But, no, she wasn't the least bit fazed. Her tongue flicked out and she licked the part he'd just bitten into.

"Mmm." She winked seductively. "Now I have boy cooties. Guess we'll have cooties together."

"I guess so," he smiled, turned on by her antics.

Duke whimpered.

"Don't worry," Katie said, pushing up the remainder of the ice cream for the puppy to lick, "we haven't forgotten you."

A few minutes later, they rounded a corner and came upon a pond where a group of picnickers were feeding bread to a flock of hungry ducks.

The minute Duke caught scent of the waterfowl, he went berserk. The cocker spaniel jerked on the leash, almost yanking Katie off her feet.

Liam grabbed for her elbow but she was already

gone, pulled toward the water by the feisty Duke, who no longer looked so regal with his teeth bared, issuing a bark so commanding it sounded as if it could have come from a Doberman.

The picnickers gawked.

The ducks scattered.

Katie tried pulling on the leash, but apparently Duke held an entrenched hatred of ducks. The mild tugging on his neck wasn't enough to stop his forward motion.

Liam sprinted after them.

Duke hit the water with a loud smack.

Katie teetered on the bank, holding tightly to the leash.

"Let go," Liam called.

But his warning came too late. The heel of her right boot was wedged between two pathway stones. She jerked backward in an attempt to extract herself, but the dog was swimming in the opposite direction.

The next thing Liam knew, a bootless Katie was tumbling headfirst into the water.

6

KATIE CAME UP sputtering. She shoved wet hair from her eyes and looked up to see Liam on the bank laughing his ass off.

"Very funny," she growled.

"It's kind of funny," he said, but at least he made an effort to stop laughing.

"I'm soaking wet."

She raised an arm. It was only then, as she watched Liam's gaze hone in on her breasts, that she realized when wet, her sweater was practically transparent. Instantly, she crossed her arms over her chest, hiding her silhouetted breasts.

He held out a hand.

If she uncrossed her arms to take his hand, he would have an extremely good view of her nipples gone hard in the cold. Oh, why had she worn a camisole today instead of a bra?

"Take my hand," he invited.

She didn't want to, but it was going to be darn difficult getting out of the muck without a boost up. Reluctantly, she took his hand and tried not to notice when he watched her nipples pebble.

"Where's Duke?" she asked, teeth chattering.

"You sit." He led Katie to a park bench and draped his suit jacket around her. The now familiar scent of him surrounded her like a welcome hug.

He retrieved her boot from where she'd lost it, then got down on one knee and slipped it onto her foot. Talk about a Cinderella complex.

"Duke," she repeated. "Three-hundred-dollar deposit."

"I'll go find him."

He returned a few minutes later with a scraggly, squirming, soaking wet Duke tucked under his arm. Liam took one look at Katie and shook his head. "You can't go back to work like that."

"I'm blaming this on you." She grinned at him, not the least bit mad.

"Me?"

"I would never have thought to rent Duke out for a walk. I guess I'm an all-or-nothing kind of woman."

"Okay, I accept full responsibility. Let's take Duke back to the pet shop and I'll drive you to my apartment. It's just a few blocks from here. I can send your clothes out to the one-hour dry cleaner in my building, while you take a shower. I'll let Max know that we'll need to postpone the meeting for another time."

Katie could have told him that her own condo wasn't far away, either, but she didn't. Bad as it sounded, she wanted to see the inside of his apartment. In fact, her heart was thumping eagerly and quickly.

She soon found herself riding in the elevator with him up to the penthouse of James Towers. She might have come from old money, but overall, she'd lead a very sheltered life. Her parents had been quite strict when she and her sisters were growing up, and it was only since college that Katie had really stretched her wings. She'd never been to a penthouse apartment before, alone, with a man she barely knew.

Her stomach tightened, sending sexy messages shooting straight to the most feminine parts of her. She tried to ignore the sensations, but she knew she was in serious trouble.

Remember the new leaf? No more meaningless sex.

Yeah, but what about the Martini dare she'd drawn the night before?

You don't have to do it.

But that was the thing. She wanted to do it.

When they stepped inside his living space and she got a bird's-eye view of downtown Boston from his wide, curtainless window, Katie forgot to breathe.

Incredible.

"Bathroom's down the hall, first door on your right," Liam announced, tossing his car keys on a table in the foyer.

The penthouse was straight out of *Architectural Digest.* Sleek, modern and totally staged. The place was devoid of any personal touches. As far as she could tell, there wasn't a bit of the real Liam here.

It made her feel a little sad to think he lived in such a sterile environment.

Katie slipped his jacket from her shoulders and draped it over a black leather couch. It was only then that she caught him watching her with heavily lidded eyes as he took in the way her damp clothes molded against her body.

Quickly, she turned and beat a hasty retreat, desperately searching for the bathroom and some small shred of self-control. She locked the bathroom door and sank against it with a shaky sigh.

He knocked on the door and she jumped, hand to her heart.

"Yes?"

"Put on my bathrobe," he said, "It's hanging on the back of the door. And then hand me out your clothes. I'll pop them down to the dry cleaner's while you shower."

Katie stripped off her clothes. She thought of his long, strong masculine fingers touching her garments and she shivered at the image.

Stop thinking like this.

She put on his bathrobe that smelled of sandalwood shampoo, opened the door a crack and thrust her things at him.

"Thank you," he said.

Why in God's name did that sound like a come-on? It was just a simple thank-you.

Cold shower, cold shower. Get in, get washed off, get out.

She did exactly that. Five minutes later, she was showered and wrapped in his bathrobe again. She took the time to rinse her undergarments out in his sink, then drape them over his shower-curtain rod. Then she searched the bathroom for a blow-dryer, but couldn't find one.

"Liam," she called, leaving the bathroom, her wet hair twisted up in a towel, and padded into the living room. "Where do you keep your blow—"

He was standing in the middle of room, stripped bare to the waist.

"What are you doing?" she asked.

He turned and a wicked grin tilted up the corners of his mouth. "Duke got me a bit wet and muddy, too."

"Well, could you cover up or something?"

"What's the matter?" He strolled toward her. "You don't like what you see?"

"No, no—" she cleared her throat "—I like. Too much." She waved a hand. "Now, cover up, please."

The muscle in his throat jumped as his eyes traveled the length of her body.

He came closer.

Katie backed up until her butt hit the wall. "Um," she said. "What are you doing?"

"What I've wanted to do all afternoon."

"It's not a good idea," she whispered as his mouth dipped closer.

"No?"

There didn't seem to be enough air in the room. You'd think in a condo this expensive there would be enough air in the flipping room. And his brownish green bedroom eyes were smothering her with closeness.

Her heart thundered at the feral look in his gaze.

He wanted her.

And she wanted him. Wanted his sweet, moist lips on hers and his masculine tongue thrusting deep inside her heated mouth.

Not only was there not enough air, but it was way too hot in here. Sizzling, in fact. It was a downright devil den.

He took her in his arms and pulled her up tight

against his bare chest. Her pulse galloped madly. She wasn't so sure about this. Things were suddenly slipping rapidly out of her control.

"I..." She started to say that she didn't think this was such a great idea, but she got no further.

His mouth came down on hers for real and it tasted good.

That night at the masquerade ball had been exciting and wild and quick, but this was different. This was up close and personal and lingering, with no disguises to hide behind. She had time to really savor his kiss. To taste cinnamon on his tongue and smell his deeply masculine scent.

Liam's tongue seared hers. She had no idea a kiss could be so intense. The towel came unwrapped from around her hair, falling slowly to the floor. Liam pushed his fingers through the damp strands, cradling her head in his hands.

Katie felt as if her entire body had short-circuited. Her stomach jolted. Her lips parted. Her toes curled. Her eyes widened.

Delight detonated in her mouth. A wildfire rolled through her nerve endings. He was suddenly more essential to her than the air she'd craved earlier.

How unforgettable he tasted. How safe she felt in his arms. It was strange to feel this way considering the circumstances, but that was how it was. As if he could and would protect her from anything.

She wanted to make love to him so badly her insides throbbed.

He tightened his arms around her. She relaxed her

jaw, and his tongue speared deep inside. Moaning softly, she slid her arms around his neck.

More, she had to have more.

His chest was hard muscle against her soft breasts. She ran her fingers through his hair and made a fist. He growled low in his throat and used his hand to trace her spine to the small of her back. Then, through the cloth of his bathrobe, he gently kneaded her backside.

Her body, which seconds before had been tense and resistant, turned fluid and supple at his touch. She was clay—pliant and malleable. Anything he asked of her she would willingly do.

Wait a minute, whispered the voice in the back of her head, *what about turning over a new leaf? What about no longer rushing in headlong where angels feared to tread?*

Right. As if she could slam the brakes on when Liam was kissing her like this.

Don't you want to be something more than everybody's good-time girl? Aren't you afraid this will jeopardize your working relationship? Or that you could lose your job over this?

Nah, she didn't care about any of that. All she cared about was the magic of this moment.

And you wonder why no one takes you seriously.

But Liam took her seriously. He'd made her art director of his ad campaign.

Maybe that's just because he was hoping to get into your panties.

Hush.

Determinedly shoving the ugly little nay-saying

voice aside, she closed her eyes, made her mind blank and inhaled him.

She explored his mouth, taste by taste, texture by texture, layer by layer. He tasted honest and clean. His flavor was all masculine substance—solid and efficient.

Katie had to hand it to him. He was one helluva great kisser.

His lips soared her higher, flying her to a glorious realm where fantasy and reality merged into frenetic excitement.

He tasted like summer vacation, like long, hot nights in the backseat of a big old American car. Like Fourth of July fireworks—dazzling and explosive. He tasted like hard work and commitment and trustworthiness. His taste made her feel safe and supported and honored.

He kissed with the power and authority of a man completely in control of himself. And she realized his self-control frightened her because she had no control of her own. He scared her because she found herself wanting something she could not even identify. Something she'd never wanted before.

His lips hummed with strength and go-getter magnetism. His kiss whispered of all that could exist between them if she just had the courage to close her hand and make a fist. To take a tentative step toward something more than fun and frivolity.

She wished she could frame this moment in time, hold on to it like a snapshot. Kiss him on and on and on forever.

The thought jolted her. This quick jog on the wild side had landed her in mental quicksand. Should she flail around and try to get free? Or should she embrace the fall?

Suddenly, the struggle was taken out of her hands.

Liam broke the kiss, pulled back, stared down at her.

"What?" she whispered, peering up into his eyes. "What's wrong?"

He stroked his index finger down the length of her jaw, then stopped and pressed his thumb against her lips. "We have to stop now, or I won't be able to stop."

"Why stop?" she asked as the weight of his thumb caressed her cheek.

He drew in a ragged breath. "Our first time together was sex-crazed and anonymous. I want us to take our time and to get to know each other before we do this again."

"But I like sex-crazed and anonymous."

He had one arm around her waist, one hand tilting her chin up to meet his gaze. He was looking at her as if she were special, like something to be treasured. No man had ever looked at her like that before. Katie held a breath.

"That might be the case," he said. "But you deserve so much more. No matter how much I might want to, I'm not going to have sex with you again."

"You're not?" Why did it feel as if he were denying her keys to Shangri-La?

"No." He shook his head. "Not now. Not yet. Not until I know everything there is to know about you."

She laughed because she didn't know what else to do.

"I'm serious," he said.

One look in his eyes told her it was true. She felt a rush of panic so strong that if she hadn't been naked underneath his bathrobe, she would have bolted straight out the front door.

But the ringing phone saved her from replying.

He let her go, easing his arm from around her waist and stepped to the cordless phone docked on the glass end table beside his leather couch.

"Yes," he answered. "Okay, thanks. Please send someone up with them." He ended the conversation, turned back to her. "That was the dry cleaner's downstairs. Your clothes are ready."

Yes!

"Here's what's going to happen," he said with the same take-charge manner she assumed he used to run his real-estate empire. "You're getting dressed and I'm driving you back to Sharper Designs. Because I have an appointment at three, I won't be able to review your designs for the ad campaign. With that in mind, I'll pick you up tomorrow night at eight for a business dinner meeting. So have your proposal ready."

"I have plans," she said, just to be ornery. She didn't have any plans beyond her usual Saturday-night clubbing, but she balked at being ordered around. Even if it was by the most eligible bachelor in Boston.

"Then cancel them."

"I ACTED LIKE a self-important, arrogant ass," Liam confided to Tony as they jogged together in the park on Saturday morning.

"She got to you, so you reacted out of instinct. Doing what you do best. Taking charge, bossing people around. It works on the job, not so great when it comes to romance."

"I can't explain it, but something about that woman brings out the caveman in me."

"You feel protective of her."

"Yeah."

"And you can't stand the thought of her dating someone else."

"Yes," Liam admitted through gritted teeth. The mere thought of some other man touching Katie twisted him inside out.

"She drives you so crazy you can't think."

"Exactly!"

Tony chuckled.

"What? It's not funny. It's irritating."

"You're falling for her."

"I'm not," he denied hotly. "It's just that she's so damned sexy."

"So have a casual fling with her."

"I tried. I couldn't go through with it."

"Why not?"

"She looked so vulnerable. Like she trusted me completely. She doesn't know me. She shouldn't trust me so easily."

"Why do you care?"

"She has no idea how terrific she is," Liam huffed as they rounded the home stretch of their five-mile run. "As an artist and as a woman. You should see her graphic designs. Amazing."

"What's she like?"

"She takes chances. I like that about her. She's upbeat and energetic and full of surprises. Lively, spontaneous, freewheeling."

"In short, all the things you aren't."

Liam dodged a park bench. "Yeah."

"So what do you want from her?"

Good question. One he'd spent the night pondering as he'd tossed and turned and remembered their incredible kisses.

"Sex?" Tony asked.

"For sure."

"But you want something more or you would have just done that again."

"Maybe," he admitted.

"Commitment?"

"Hey, wait, slow down. Slow way, way down. All I'm saying is that she's interested me more than any woman has in a long time." *If ever.*

"So you're looking for a little romance? Nothing more than a good time."

"Yeah, I suppose so."

"But you don't really know how to romance a girl because you've spent your entire adult life getting ahead, amassing your fortune. And when you've had relationships in the past, it was up to the woman to put forth all the effort to keep you interested."

"Something like that."

Tony hooted. "I love it. Now you're sweating because you're scared that *you're* not exciting enough for *her.*"

His best friend had seen right through him, but he was loath to admit it. "Don't be ridiculous."

"Wanna know how to keep her interested?"

"No." *Yes, yes!*

"I'll tell you because I know you're only saying no to save face."

"I am not," he lied.

"You keep her guessing."

"Guessing?"

"I know it's hard for you to wrap your one-track mind around this concept, but to keep a fun-loving woman like Katie entertained, you've got to be unpredictable."

"Unpredictable?"

"You know, do something impromptu, unexpected. Send her a gift no one else would ever send her. Something that would have special meaning for her. Take her someplace you would normally never go, like to a monster-truck rally."

"A monster-truck rally?" Liam snorted. "That's the best you have to offer?"

"Okay, that was a stab in the dark, but use your imagination. Take her salsa dancing. Or kayaking. Or ice skating. Have fun."

"Fun?"

"You know, the thing you haven't done since you were a kid." Tony eyed him as they jogged side by side. "But this isn't the kind of woman who's going to be impressed by fancy French restaurants or long-stemmed red roses and boxes of chocolates."

"Too predictable?"

"By far. Convincing her you're good for anything more than a hot time between the sheets is going to take some thought and effort on your part."

Liam blew out his breath. "You make it sound like I don't stand a chance."

"She's going to be a challenge for you, but come on. When have you ever shied away from a challenge? Just put the same effort into pursuing Katie that you've always put into buying and selling property then you'll be A-OK. Throw the woman a curve ball or two."

Easy enough for him to say, Tony knew how to chill out and have a good time. Liam was fighting against thirty-one years of hard work and determination to get ahead at all costs.

Think, think. What can you do to delight Katie? What will keep her guessing?

Just as they finished the last leg of their run, inspiration hit. Liam knew exactly what he was going to send that would both intrigue and surprise her.

MAKE LOVE in a forbidden place.

Katie read the Martini dare she'd tucked into the corner of her dresser mirror as she sat at her vanity wrapping her hair around a curling iron.

She'd been anxious all afternoon getting ready for this business dinner with Liam. She'd gone to the mall, bought a new dress and new pair of shoes. She'd had a manicure and a facial. She skipped both breakfast and lunch because she was too nervous to eat. She was acting as if it were a date.

It is a date.

No, it was a business meeting.

So then how come no one else on the creative team was invited?

Yeah, why was that?

He wants you, you want him, go for it.

"But I'm turning over a new leaf. Giving up casual sex, going cold turkey," Katie said aloud to her reflection.

And then her gaze strayed to the parchment again. *Make love in a forbidden place.*

Why did it have to be cold turkey? Why couldn't she sort of taper off? Plenty of people used the patch to wean themselves off smoking. Couldn't the three Martini dares serve as Katie's swan song for casual sex?

Liam was the perfect person to perform her dares with, she convinced herself. They were attracted to each other. He was temporary, only in her life for as long as it took to oversee the graphic designs for his campaign. Plus, they'd already made love, so by continuing their affair she was actually taking it out of the realm of one-night stands.

She loosened her grip on the curling iron and the warm curl escaped to fall gently across her cheek. She picked up a second strand of hair and twisted it around the heated rod.

The memory of what had happened in his apartment the afternoon before popped into her head. She remembered the feel of his lips, the pleasure of his tongue.

And then she thought of the way he'd looked at her. No, not at her...into her, as if he could see straight to her soul. Past the wild-child image she projected. Past the carefree persona she'd perfected. Past the clothes and the parties and jokes to the wounded woman who'd lost both her parents before she was twenty-five. To the girl who'd always felt as if she had to show others a good time in order to be loved and appreciated.

Katie shivered and pushed that disturbing thought away. She didn't want to examine it too closely. She had other things on her mind.

Make love in a forbidden place.

"I'll do it," she whispered to her reflection in the mirror. "I'm going to use Liam to complete my Martini dares."

Just saying the words made her feel empowered. Yes. This was good. This was exactly what she was looking for.

But is it fair to use Liam for your own personal empowerment?

The doorbell rang, interrupting her internal seesaw. She turned off the curling iron, got up and padded to the door. She peered through the peephole and spied a bike messenger standing on her front step. She put the chain on and opened the door a crack.

"Special delivery," he called. "You gotta sign for it."

What was this? Katie was a city girl who knew how to take care of herself. "Who's it from?"

"Mr. Liam James."

Magic words.

Katie signed for the package, then almost ripped it out of the delivery guy's hands. Her curiosity was piqued. What had Liam sent her?

She tore off the brown paper to reveal a rectangular white box with the name of a famous jewelry store embossed in red letters on the lid. Her heart thumped.

Jewelry? The gift was presumptuous. Jewelry implied strings were attached to their relationship and she certainly wasn't interested in getting tied to anything. She suddenly felt claustrophobic, as if the walls of her condo were closing in.

Maybe she should reconsider her decision to use Liam as the means to complete her Martini dares.

Tentatively, she slid the lid off the box and peered inside to find…

A dog collar?

The dude had sent her a dog collar.

Albeit a very handsome dog collar. Made of black leather and studded with blue onyx and faux diamond rhinestones. When she lifted it out of the box, the stones glistened in the light.

At the bottom of the box lay a small card. She plucked it out and read the message that had been printed in strong, masculine block script.

Dear Katie,

For when you're ready to claim Duke as your own. Looking forward to seeing you tonight.

Liam

P.S. You'd make a terrific dog owner.

A dog collar for a puppy she didn't even own? It was a strange gift, but she found the gesture incredibly touching because Liam had paid attention. And he'd understood both her desire to own a dog and her anxiety over such a commitment.

A wistful feeling swept over her—part longing, and part…*hope.*

The fact that Liam had gone to all the trouble to pick out this dog collar and have it couriered over stirred something deep. He could have sent generic flowers or candy or nothing at all. But instead, he'd sent the one thing that said *I believe in you.*

She was moved.

The gift spoke volumes. Clearly, tonight was not just a business meeting.

Katie had a date with Boston's most eligible bachelor.

7

"THANK YOU for the dog collar," Katie told Liam when he came to pick her up. "It was very thoughtful."

"I wanted to encourage you to get that puppy, if that's what you really want."

"I don't know that I want a dog *that* badly, but thanks for the vote of confidence."

"Don't want it? Or too afraid to want it?" Liam challenged.

Damn, being with this guy wasn't easy. He didn't let her slide on anything. She darted a quick glance at him. He was standing in her foyer, gorgeous as all get-out.

He wore a black pullover V-necked sweater and a pair of formfitting black trousers. The wind had sexily tousled his well-groomed hair, giving him a relaxed look she found appealing.

Her gaze tracked over his face, soaking up his chiseled cheekbones and strong chin. She noticed that the bridge of his nose was crooked, bent slightly to the right as if once it had been broken.

Liam looked so different from the pampered playboys she normally dated. His life experience was evident not only in the sharp focus of his intelligent hazel eyes and the out-of-character tattoo at his left wrist, but also in the powerful way he carried himself, in the commanding way he spoke.

This was a man of substance.

She was surprised to find the observation made her edgy. Very edgy. Suddenly, all her self-confidence evaporated. What did she know about pleasing a high-powered businessman who'd bootstrapped his way to the top of his profession by age thirty? And she was a woman who'd been born with a blue-blooded spoon in her mouth.

His standards were high. He was a self-made millionaire, well on his way to becoming a billionaire. He was everything she was not. Logical, responsible, dedicated, driven.

Was that why he fascinated her so? Because she could never hope to understand what made him tick?

A smile tipped his lips and as his eyes met hers, his face lit up. He looked as if the Dow Jones had jumped twenty points.

Katie's heart fluttered. He had the power to make her feel special. It was disconcerting, to say the least.

"Wow, you look amazing." The appreciative expression in his eyes went a long way in reviving her poise and earning him bonus points for noticing the special care that she'd taken with her appearance.

Approvingly, his gaze traveled from her fresh new hairstyle, across the swell of the tight bodice of her aqua dress to the hemline that hit her midthigh to the three-inch stilettos that enhanced the shapely curve of her lean legs.

Noticing everything. Missing nothing. Making her feel very desirable.

"Thank you," she said, and tried not to blush at his frank assessment.

"Are you ready to get down to business?" His hazel eyes smoldered with a mesmerizing sexuality that pushed all the air from her lungs.

"Business?"

"You do have your designs with you."

"Yes, yes," she said breathlessly. Oh, she'd almost forgotten about the designs.

"Good," he said. "I can't wait to see what you've come up with."

"I hope you like them."

"I have confidence in you." He winked.

He took her to Carmine's Ristorante, a quaint family-owned Italian restaurant off the beaten path, but not far from Boston's north end. It wasn't the sort of place she expected a real-estate mogul to frequent. That alone impressed her.

He'd opened the door for her, lightly placing his hand at the small of her back to guide her over the threshold.

The pressure of his hand had her sucking in her breath. She didn't know what to make of his proprietary touch or the way her skin tingled.

Her pulse leaped and instantly a dozen erotic images from the night of the Ladies League ball popped into her head. She heard the clatter of coat hangers, the sounds of their delighted groans. She smelled the scent of their merged bodies, musky and rich. She tasted the sweet flavor of sin on her tongue.

"Hello, Mr. James," greeted the attractive, overeager young hostess. "We've got your usual table waiting."

The hostess led them through the brightly lit dining room to a table in the corner. Katie wondered if he often brought dates here. It didn't seem like a regular date place. No singing waiters. No candles in Chianti bottles. No private booths to hide away from the crowd. Most of the tables seated six or more and they all seemed to be filled with families or groups of coworkers or friends on an outing.

Maybe this really was a business meeting.

The man was sending mixed messages and she wasn't sure how to read him. Her interest notched higher. Who was Liam James behind his reputation and his stunning success? What had made him the man he was today?

"I hope this place is okay," he said anxiously. "It's not trendy, but the owner and his family are friendly and the food is great."

He was trying so hard in that moment, as if her approval meant a lot. *He's as nervous as I am,* she realized with a start. She was touched that he cared enough to be nervous.

"Did the *Young Bostonian* article drive you underground?" she said. "Or do you always prefer to frequent out-of-the-way places?"

"You saw that article," he said, pulling her chair out for her.

She sat down and slid her briefcase under the table. "Oh, indeed. Who could miss it? Impressive piece about Boston's premiere hotshot multimillionaire. You've got the buzz, babe."

He sat down across from her. A look of embarrassment crossed his face. "It's a lot of hype."

"Somehow I doubt that."

The waiter came over. Liam ordered a bottle of modestly priced white wine and antipasto as an appetizer. He wasn't trying to impress her. Why not?

Katie was confused. She knew he was attracted to her, but he wasn't pulling out all the stops. What was the deal?

The waiter returned with their wine and the antipasto plate heaped with buffalo mozzarella, salami, black olives, sun-dried tomato relish and thin slices of toasted garlic-bread rounds.

"Are you ready to order your main course?" the waiter asked.

"Oops," Katie said. "I haven't even looked at the menu." Because she'd been too busy looking at Liam.

"They have excellent veal marsala," he suggested.

"Veal marsala it is," she said, and passed her menu to the waiter and thanked him.

Once the waiter had gone, she leaned in closer. The scent of Liam's cologne mingled with the delicious smell of the antipasto. It was a bracing fragrance, hearty and substantial. "Thank you for bringing me here. I adore Italian food. It's my favorite."

"Mine, too."

Strange. She'd pegged him as a sushi lover or maybe upscale French cuisine. Mr. *Young Bostonian,* and all that.

"Why don't we take a look at the mock-ups while we eat?" she said. "Kill two birds with one stone."

"Actually," he said, reaching across the table to rest his hand on hers to stop her from reaching for her briefcase, "I have a confession to make."

"A confession?" She studied him, still thrown by the mixed messages he was sending. It wasn't often that any male knocked her off-kilter.

Using the food as an excuse, she slipped her hand out from under his and reached for a toast round, scooping a spoonful of the sun-dried tomato relish onto the garlic bread.

"This dinner isn't strictly business."

"No?" She chased the antipasto with a measured swallow of wine but never took her gaze from his face.

"Surely you knew it was pretext." His smile was positively wicked and spiked up the heat already invading Katie's body. "We could have had the business meeting at Sharper Designs on Monday."

They stared at each other across the table.

"Listen," they said in unison, then both broke off, chuckling.

"Why don't you go ahead and show me the designs you've come up with?" Liam said. "Let's get the business portion of this meeting over with so we can—"

"Get down to the pleasure?" Katie impishly finished for him.

"That wasn't what I was going to say."

"No," she countered, "I'm certain you'd planned on being much more diplomatic."

"You think I'm a stuffed shirt?"

"I think that's the image you portray, but I know better. I've seen the real you in action."

His face flushed. "You're referring to the Ladies League ball."

"I am." She lowered her eyelashes.

"That's not the real me. You just caught me on a bad night."

"Not from my point of view." She winked. "I thought you were very, very good that night."

His Adam's apple bobbed as he swallowed. "I took advantage of you."

"That's not the way I recall it. In my memory, I clearly took advantage of you."

"Either way, it was a life-altering experience for me."

"How's that?"

"Ever since that night I've been unable to think about anything but you."

"*Really?*" she said.

"Believe me, that's not normal."

"Way to flatter a girl," she teased, "telling her it's not normal to be wanted."

"That's not what I mean…" He pressed a palm to the back of his neck, chuffed out a breath. "I'm handling this badly."

She studied his face, clean-shaven, honest, above-board. If this had been the Middle Ages, he most certainly would have been a dutiful knight, stalwart and well-intentioned.

Something scary shifted inside her. Maybe she shouldn't try her Martini dare on him. He was too nice of a guy and she didn't want to hurt him. "Liam, I…"

"Yes?"

The way he was looking at her caused her feminine sex to clench with a swift squeeze of ravenous need. A deep-seated tightening of desire. She had to have him, never mind the costs.

Befuddled by lust, she dropped her gaze, fumbled blindly for her briefcase, heard her heart pounding blood rapidly through her ears. "I…I've got your proposal right here. I've gotta warn you, the designs are a bit racy, but you did say you wanted sex."

The word *sex* hung in the air, as provocative as heavy breathing.

Unnerved, Katie pushed aside the appetizer plate, scooted her chair closer so they could both see it and placed the file folder on the table between them. "Obviously we're appealing to young, urban professionals with a high income."

"Obviously," he agreed, and leaned over her shoulder. The warmth of his breath fanned the hairs along the nape of her neck.

She flipped open the file, then looked at him to gauge his initial reaction to the graphics of her mock-up.

Suddenly, she understood exactly how much she wanted his approval.

Liam tilted his head to study the photograph with interest, but his face remained unreadable. Damn him and his perfect self-control.

In the ad, a lithe young woman was stepping naked from a patio hot tub underneath a starlit sky. She was holding a white terry cloth towel in her hand that barely covered her explicit parts.

Seated on a lawn chair, in the dark, at the far end of the patio was a man equally as naked, his explicit bits hidden in the shadow cast by a glistening chrome barbecue grill. The man's eyes were hooked on the woman, the unmistakable signs of feral lust on his face.

The woman was as blond as Katie, the man as dark-haired as Liam. The setting was totally intimate. The choice of models and setting had not been accidental. She'd worked very hard to create an erotic, atmospheric draft that was still subtle enough for mainstream media. It had been a tricky balance, getting the right play of light, capturing the seductive interplay without going over the top.

"We're thinking of a caption along the lines of— James Place Condominiums…Where Your Most Forbidden Fantasies Come True," she said. "But the copywriters are still working on it."

He raised his gaze from the photo, locked eyes with her. "It makes me want to sell my penthouse apartment and move in tomorrow."

"You really like it?" His approval gladdened her heart.

"It's exceptional work. You've accurately captured exactly what I was going for. The color, the mood, the marketing elements. You're a master at this, Katie. You can go as high as you want in your career."

The way he was looking at her made her feel competent and accomplished and reliable. She could honestly say no one else had ever made her feel quite this proud of her work. Katie wasn't accustomed to impressing a man with her artistic skills, especially a man with as much business savvy as this one. He made her want to truly commit to her career. To throw herself into it the same way she threw herself into romantic adventures.

It was a new experience, this desire to be industrious and self-reliant. She liked it.

And she liked him.

Then he did something completely unexpected.

Liam reached over, took her hand in his, stared deeply into her eyes and said, "After dinner, would you like to go bowling?"

BOWLING?

Why in the hell had he invited her to go bowling? Liam had never bowled a day in his life.

Why? Because Tony had advised him to throw her a few curveballs. And his friend's advice had seemed to work with the dog collar and taking her to Carmine's when his instincts had been to send long-stemmed roses and take her to the fanciest French restaurant in town in a limo.

But bowling? Maybe he should have given the monster-truck rally more consideration.

Unfortunately for him, Katie had been excited at his suggestion. Apparently the girl loved to bowl. Who could have suspected a well-bred Brahmin blue blood would go for bowling?

The alley was alive with noise. He was seriously out of his element as he laced up the two-toned rented shoes. Why on earth was he doing this? His forte was the boardroom, not the bowling lanes.

Then he looked at Katie with her face aglow and he knew why. Her smile made him happy. The realization surprised him. The happiness surprised him.

Absentmindedly, he raised a palm and pressed it against his heart as he watched her pick up her bowling ball and take aim at the ten pins. She looked adorable in those ugly bowling shoes, the hem of her dress swirling around her firm thighs and her hair tumbling over her shoulders in untamed abandon.

He loved her gung-ho spirit and her lively personality. She could turn something as mundane as taking out the trash into a grand adventure. Life with Katie would be lots of fun.

Trouble was, Liam wasn't used to fun. If he wasn't working, he felt guilty for leaving things undone. He hadn't made it where he was today by goofing off with frivolous activities such as bowling.

Being with Katie made him understand how much he'd been missing out on. And he was tired of missing out. Even if it meant he had to make a fool of himself at the bowling alley.

She bent over to take the shot.

Underneath his palm, he felt his heart rate kick up.

She wiggled her butt and he couldn't help but think she was teasing him. Then she was in motion, floating gracefully down the lane as only a bowling, blue-blooded princess could. She let go of the ball. It rolled down the alley, mowing down every pin.

"Strike!" she yelled gleefully, and spun around toward him, a huge smile on her face. She came trotting over to where he sat. "High five."

He slapped her upraised palm. The smacking sound, the resulting tingle as his flesh met hers, caused a stirring deep inside him. A stirring unlike anything he'd ever felt before. He had no name for it and that bothered him.

Her gaze met his. Nervously, she flicked out a tongue to lick her lips. It wasn't a calculated gesture, of that he was sure. But the sight of her sweet pink tongue darting out to moisten those full red lips caused his stomach to contract and his penis to harden.

"Where'd you learn to bowl like that?" he asked. "Last time I checked they don't have bowling alleys in Beacon Hill."

"My mother," she said.

"Bowling isn't a sport that high-society mamas usually encourage their daughters to take up."

"My mother was an exceptional woman."

"I've got to hand it to her. She certainly raised an exceptional daughter," he said.

Katie smiled at his compliment and he discovered he felt quite pleased to bring that smile to her face. "Mom did a lot of things with us you wouldn't expect from a woman with her advantages and privileges. Sometimes, it earned her criticism from my dad's family."

"What about your mom's family?" he asked.

"Her parents had passed away and she didn't have any siblings."

"What about cousins?" he asked. "Aunts or uncles?"

"That was always sort of a mystery," Katie admitted. "My mother never talked about her extended family. My sisters and I got the impression she was estranged from them. We didn't really ask about it. My father's family was so close-knit."

"What else did your mother like to do besides bowl?"

"Ice skate, bicycling, anything active. She even took us go-carting one time. I loved it, but Joey fell out of her cart and skinned her knees. Dad forbid any more go-cart excursions after that."

"It sounds as if you and your mother were a lot alike," he commented.

Katie looked surprised by the suggestion. "I hadn't really thought of it that way, but, yeah, maybe so. We were the two who never seemed to fit in with the Winfields."

"Tell me more about your family."

"Don't think I don't know what you're up to. You're the kind of guy who hates to lose and you've seen what a whiz I am on the lanes. No more stalling. It's your turn. Get out there."

"But I'm enjoying getting to know you better." He patted the hard vinyl seat next to him.

"What's the matter?" she taunted. "Are you afraid you can't live up to my strike?"

"Absolutely."

"Get up." She reached out, took him by the hand and hauled him to his reluctant feet.

"Bowling's really not my strong suit."

"I promise, I won't gloat when I beat your pants off."

"I don't believe you. You seem like the type who would gloat over her prowess," he teased.

She raised two fingers. "Promise."

"Here's the deal. I've got a confession to make," he said as she tugged him toward the lane.

"Oh?"

"I can't bowl."

She canted her head. "Quit stalling and get out there."

"No, honestly, I can't bowl."

"Really?"

He shrugged.

She rested her hands on her hips. "Then why did you suggest we come here?"

"I was hoping to surprise you with a fun activity you wouldn't expect me to suggest."

"And you did."

"I had no clue you had the makings of a pro bowler. I thought we could look silly together. Now you're just going to mop the floor with me."

Katie giggled. "Don't be afraid to look silly. No one cares, honestly. Just pick up your ball and take your best shot."

He walked to the ball carousel, stopped, turned back to look at her. Damn, but she seemed to be taking an inordinate amount of glee in his ineptitude.

"Come on, where's the fearless attitude that propelled you to king of the heap of Boston real estate? I know you've got a risk-taking gene in there somewhere."

"It only applies to business."

"I don't believe that."

He couldn't fight her infectious smile. "All right," he conceded, "I'll try."

"That's all I can ask."

Liam picked up the ball, figured out where to slip his fingers into the holes and then walked to the edge of the lane. How exactly did this thing work? He sneaked a peek at the bowlers on the next lane over.

"Use the arrows on the floor to line up your shot," Katie called out.

He looked over his shoulder. "I don't—"

"What? You don't ask for help?"

"Not until I've exhausted all other options." He grinned.

She sat back against the plastic seating, knees crossed, one leg bouncing provocatively and sent him a wicked grin. "Stubborn."

"A man likes to do things his own way."

"Even if it's the hard way?"

"Uh-huh."

"Tough guy going it alone, huh? No need to be part of the pack. Lone wolf Liam."

"Something like that."

"Sounds desolate to me."

"Yeah," he admitted with a cheerful shake of his head, "maybe a little."

"Fine. Go it alone." She chuckled. "I'll keep my advice to myself."

"Thank you," he said, and promptly threw a gutter ball.

Katie hooted.

He sauntered toward her. "I suppose I deserved that."

"Darn right."

One look into her eyes and nothing mattered except keeping that wide smile on her face. He kept forgetting he'd hired her to advertise his condos, that she was essentially his employee. As they bowled frame after frame—or rather, she bowled and he pitched balls down the gutter—Liam found himself wanting her more and more. And by the time they ended up at her front door, he couldn't keep his hands off her.

All evening her laughter had pealed like wind chimes in his imagination, light and free. Whenever she brushed against him, an uncontrollable surge of hormones deployed straight to his loins. And when he drew close to her, he smelled the exotic scent of her shampoo—a piquant blend of lotus blossoms and crystal ginger. It was all he could do to keep himself from burying his nose in her shimmering hair.

"Thanks for a wonderful time," she said. "I know this was supposed to be a business meeting, not a real date, but I had more fun than I've had in a long while."

"Me, too," he said huskily.

She turned to slip her key into the lock.

He put his arm on the doorjamb over her head. He couldn't remember the last time he'd wanted a woman this badly. "You're not going to invite me in?"

"On our first date, which wasn't even really a date?" She turned back, eyes dancing. "What kind of girl do you think I am?"

"I didn't...that wasn't...um..."

"Lighten up, silly," she said, "I was just yanking your chain."

"Oh."

"But I'm not inviting you in."

"Why not?"

"Because," she said, "I've got something better in mind."

His curiosity was piqued. "What's that?"

She wagged a finger. "If I told you, it would take all the fun out of it."

"You are a tease." He couldn't stop looking at her sweet mouth. At his perusal, her lips parted like petals opening.

"Guilty as charged."

"And remorseless in what you're doing to me."

"Where's the fun in remorse?"

She winked. He loved the way her conspiratorial winks made him feel as they shared a gigantic secret. She looked adorable—grinning up at him, hair tousled, dimples dug deep in her cheeks.

To hell with self-control, to hell with restraint. He'd spent too many years holding back where his love life was concerned. He took a step closer.

She reached up to tuck a hank of hair behind one ear.

"I'm going to kiss you," he announced.

She placed her index fingers to her lips. "No, not tonight. Wait."

"Wait for what?" Impatience tugged at him. He didn't want to wait. He wanted her now.

"Our secret rendezvous."

"What secret rendezvous?"

"The one we're going to have on Monday afternoon during your lunch hour."

"I usually work on my lunch hour."

"But you won't," she said. "Not this Monday."

"And why not?"

"Because I have something totally erotic in store for you." She touched the tip of her tongue to her upper lip and arched against his body. "You're going to meet me in front of the Town Crier Theatre in the historical district at noon."

He was hard for her instantly, mindless with desire. He could barely take in air, much less swallow past the cast-iron lump in his throat. "And what," he croaked, "will we be doing?"

"Come prepared—" she said the word soft and slow "—to do the forbidden."

8

COME PREPARED to do the forbidden.

Katie's scintillating parting comment echoed in his head. Did she have any idea how totally provocative those words were? Liam had lain awake all night, his brain conjuring a myriad of tantalizing possibilities. His curiosity was aroused, his blood stirred, his dormant sense of adventured stoked. His body prickled with heightened anticipation.

The woman had one hell of a creative imagination.

Just before noon on Monday afternoon, Liam paced the sidewalk outside the Town Crier Theatre wondering what delicious treats she had in store for him.

The theatre was running a weeklong retrospective of Clark Gable films. The movie du jour, according to the marquee, was *It Happened One Night*.

Fitting.

The title made him think of the one night he'd spent in the cloak closet with Katie. His mouth was dry from the memory. His hip pocket was stuffed with condoms and his anxiety was off the charts. She had him crazed with lust for her.

Five minutes passed. Then ten.

He checked his watch repeatedly. Eleven minutes. Twelve. His spirits plummeted. Had she stood him up? Or was making him wait part of her wicked game?

If that was the case, she'd won. His self-control—the thing he prided himself on most—was totally shot.

Just when Liam was about to give up and go to the office to try to get some work done, he saw her, strutting up the sidewalk toward him with the confidence of a runway model.

She was dressed all in black, which created an erotic contrast to her wheat-blond hair. She wore a tight black sweater cut so low it was barely legal and, clearly, she was not wearing a bra. The square of black leather posing as a skirt was barely bigger than a cup towel. She had on black patterned stockings and black stilettos so high it was a miracle she could walk in them.

Every guy on that Boston sidewalk was turning to stare at her.

Enthralled, Liam's jaw dropped and his pupils widened. He was desperate to see more of her. Adrenaline mixed with testosterone. The combo blasted through his veins like a fiery virus, infecting him with a level of lust the likes of which he'd never experienced.

She passed right by him. At first he thought she hadn't seen him, but then he got that it was all part of her erotic role-playing game.

Be prepared to do the forbidden.

She sashayed up to the ticket counter, bought her ticket and strolled inside without a backward look.

His cock turned to stone.

He followed suit. Buying a ticket and then following her inside the darkened theatre. At twelve o'clock on a weekday afternoon, they were the only two people in the lobby.

The theatre had been fully restored in the cinema heyday of when it had been built. The carpeting was colorful and lavishly patterned. The gold-plated lighting fixtures gleamed, polished to a high sheen. A black-and-white art-deco cat clock on the wall behind the concession stand ticked off the moments until show time. Three, two, one.

The smell of freshly popped popcorn filled the air. Katie stopped and bought a box of three-dollar jelly beans from the elderly woman behind the counter. She opened the box of candy and stood in silhouette so he could watch her pop one into her mouth and suck leisurely on it.

Liam quelled a groan.

"Would you like a sweet treat, sir?" the woman asked as Katie walked away.

"No, thanks." He shook his head. There was only one sweet treat he wanted and she was escaping.

The woman nodded, went back to perch on her stool in the corner and picked up the romance novel she'd been reading. Liam went after Katie.

She did not go in through the main entrance. Rather, she made a beeline for the marble stairs leading up into the balcony.

Thick red velvet ropes stationed on either side of the steps barred access to the lofty seating. But Katie wasn't allowing a measly stretch of cable to deter her. She winnowed around the rope, keeping to the strip of carpet running down the middle of the gray marble to blunt the sound of her high heels. She swept elegantly up the staircase.

Mesmerized, Liam flaunted the rules and tracked after her.

She pushed back the red velvet curtain leading into the balcony. He did the same, slipping past the rope. His heart suddenly was pounding so loudly he feared the noise of it would echo throughout the empty theatre and alert the staff to their clandestine rendezvous.

Once behind the curtain, he had to stop and let his eyes adjust to the darkness. The black-and-white movie was just starting, transporting them into a different era.

After a couple of seconds, he spotted her, on the back row of the empty balcony, up high, right underneath the projector, so they couldn't be spotted from the projection booth.

Excitement twisting his gut, Liam sidled up the remaining steps and eased into the seat beside her.

"Katie," he gasped.

"My name is Veronique," she whispered in a seductive French accent. "And I do not need to know yours."

He felt the blood leave his head and rush pell-mell to deliver massive doses of testosterone to his groin.

"What do you need, Veronique?" he found himself asking her huskily.

"I need adventure."

"What kind of adventure?"

"Forbidden adventure," she murmured.

Excitement trembled his hand. The scent of her invaded his nostrils. Her daring spirit clipped him hard. His muscles clenched. The tension was almost more than he could tolerate.

His eyes met hers.

In the darkness, in the heat of the moment, the black of her pupils grew so large they almost encompassed the azure blue of her irises. Was it his imagination, or were her lips trembling as much as his hands?

Foolish as it might be, he had to have her.

Liam realized how very little he knew about her, beyond the fact that she was one of *those* Winfields. The thought served to send his desire soaring.

He'd never experienced excitement like this. Not in the boardroom, not when making a fabulous deal on a piece of renovated property, not being named *Young Bostonian*'s bachelor of the year. The closest he had ever come to this sensation was when he drove his Lamborghini over the speed limit.

What a helluva ride.

A sense of rash abandon shoved him headfirst into decadence. It was not an emotion he was familiar with. Liam was normally an expert at delayed gratification. But not today. Not with this amazing woman. If he lived to be a hundred, he would never forget her.

With one slender, well-manicured finger, she raked her nail along his jawline.

Liam stifled a groan. Who knew a gentle scratch would feel so erotic? Katie's stroking brought a whole new element of awareness into play as he imagined those sweet fingers investigating other, more vulnerable areas of his body.

Her bold self-confidence inflamed him. She was a complex and complicated woman and he wanted to know everything about her. His hungry curiosity almost sent him over the brink of reason.

What did she have up her sleeve?

She'd started this seduction, this exotic tease, but damn if he wasn't committed to finishing it.

On the screen in front of them, Clark Gable flirted with Claudette Colbert, but Liam didn't notice. He had eyes for only one woman.

In the muted glow from the light of the projector, he studied Katie. She sent him a look that jammed his libido into hyperdrive, slowly licked her lips, and then leaned over the arm of her chair to lightly run that naughty tongue over his lips.

Blood, fiery and indolent, pooled in his groin. Every nerved ending leaped as electrical impulses shot through the circuitry of his brain.

The lovely Veronique tasted of licorice jelly beans and lusty woman. Their tongues tangoed. First she was the leader, muddling his senses, but then he took over, giving as good as he'd gotten. Making her mewl with escalating pleasure.

He was back in control.

Or at least he thought he was until she broke the kiss, pressed her mouth to his ear and whispered, "I'm not wearing panties."

Sweat slicked his brow, his chest, his thigh, and the pounding between his thighs intensified. His cock was damned stiff and sensitive, thrusting against the zipper of his slacks.

Shamelessly, she pressed her bosom against his arm and kissed him again, her mouth gobbling up his as if she knew every single outlaw fantasy that crossed his mind.

He brushed his hand against her breast and lightly pinched the nipple straining against the soft material. Her flesh beaded as hard as a pebble beneath his touch.

She sucked in her breath with a sex-fueled hiss. "Oh, yeah."

"That's it," he murmured, proud of his masculine prowess. "Tell me what you like."

"I want your cock." She slipped her hand down the front of his shirt to his waistband. Boldly, she eased down his zipper and reached inside.

It was his turn to hiss in his breath.

She nibbled his neck while her hand stroked his rock-hard flesh with a teasing caress. On screen, Clark was stringing up a blanket to separate him from Claudette.

Knowing that they were making out in the balcony of a movie theatre, that any minute an usher could walk in and find them, was beyond exhilarating. It was forbidden, yes, but that's what made it so awesome.

Liam felt the pulse in her wrist leap hard and fast against the head of his penis and Liam knew Katie was just as turned on as he was.

"I want you," he growled. "Now."

"Wait," she said huskily.

He felt her fumble around in the darkness, heard the sound of something being unwrapped. Condom, he thought, and then she was rolling the rubber on his burgeoning cock.

She straddled the arms of the chair he was sitting in, wrapped her hands around his neck and slowly eased herself down on the length of him. Instinctively, his hands went to span her waist, holding her in place and letting out his breath on a long, controlled exhale.

Her wet moistness engulfed him and he was inside her. "Ride me." His voice was gravel.

"My pleasure." She rode him hard and fast until they were soaring together, mindless of the noise they were making. Beyond caring who could hear.

Liam was so crazy with desire for her he couldn't stop himself. He had to do this. There was no other way out.

Their joining was quick and urgent and very, very dangerous. Everything was borderless, open. They rolled into infinity, and every blissful inch felt right and good and true. Liam couldn't distinguish who was inside whom. They were both inside, occupying the bones, skin, muscles, cells. Together, they spun.

The tasty expanse of their union multiplied, swelling beyond comprehension. A harmonious, voiceless galaxy whirling quicker than the speed of sound.

Past thinking, with no coherent thought in his head, he was nothing but cock and ass and balls.

Alive with sensation.

Relentlessly, Katie rocked into him. He was aching, gushing, throbbing. He had to bite down on his lip to keep from letting loose with a primal cry. To keep from begging for release from this glorious torture. From the rapture he could almost touch.

Tingling. Humming. Rushing.

Soon. Please, please let it be soon. It had better be or he'd implode.

And then, just like that, it was upon him.

Liam tumbled. Jerking and trembling into the abyss, hurtling. Lost. Enveloped by the chasm. The earth, the sky, the air, the ocean exploded in a ball of white-hot come.

He blinked, befuddled.

Katie collapsed. Sank her head against his.

He wrapped his arms around her and they sat there, sweating, shuddering, panting for breath.

The urgency was gone. His cock emptied. But his mind was one speeding thought after another. Adrift in a darkened world of squeaky theatre seats, red velvet curtains and the smell of buttered popcorn.

They had traveled so far together, had shared such a forbidden intimacy that when they settled back into their separate selves, a fierce melancholy fell over him.

Their lovemaking had been so remarkable that Liam did not know what to do now.

They did not know each other. Not really. They possessed no common ground. No shared history or background in which to salvage their separateness. In the confines of the old theatre, with Clark kissing Claudette on screen, they navigated unknown terrain.

Then, before he could make a move, Katie decided for him. She rose up from his lap, slipped from his grasp. "Give me a two-minute start before you follow."

Then she was gone.

Several minutes later, as Liam left the theatre on legs so shaky he was amazed he could walk, he realized that this movie would always be branded in his brain as *It Happened One Forbidden Afternoon.*

LIAM WAS SITTING in his office, scrunched down in his chair, staring out the window when a soft knock sounded and his door opened a crack.

"Liam?"

"Huh?" Liam jerked upright and blinked at his secretary Vanessa Gomez. She studied him with a look of motherly concern. "What is it?"

"I don't mean to overstep boundaries, but is there something unusual going on in your personal life?"

"Why do you ask?"

"You've been very distracted lately and your moods are all over the place." Vanessa was an impeccable employee. Forty-five, caramel-skinned, always professionally dressed and well put together. She also didn't pry into his private life, not usually. But that could have been because up until now he hadn't had much of a private life.

"Sorry, my mind was elsewhere." *On his wild lunchtime encounter with Katie.*

"On the warehouse-condo renovations?"

"Yeah," he lied, "that's it."

She crossed the room, settled some files on his desk. "These contracts need your signature."

"Thanks." He nodded.

Vanessa started to leave, but stopped at the door. "Oh, and one other thing."

"Yes?"

"Finn Delancy's secretary called from the mayor's office."

"What?" He planted both palms on his desk and shot to his feet. Irrationally, his first thought was, *He's finally calling to acknowledge he's my father.* "When?"

"Just a few minutes ago." Her eyes narrowed. "Are you sure you're okay?"

"I'm fine," Liam said curtly, his pulse pounding in his temple. "What did Delancy want?"

"Why, to invite you to a dinner party at his house. That whole *Young Bostonian* thing has the city buzzing about you. Plus, he might want to put the squeeze on you for a campaign contribution."

Here it was. A second chance to confront Delancy in public. Honestly, he'd been so wrapped up in Katie that he'd almost forgotten about his vendetta against Delancy.

Almost.

"When's the party?" he asked.

"This Wednesday at eight. Should I tell him you're available?"

Liam swallowed hard, curled his hands into fists. "You bet."

"I'll let his PA know." Vanessa headed for the door, but paused when she reached it and turned back. "Oh, he's expecting you to bring a date."

EMPOWERED BY the bold thing she'd done during her lunch hour, Katie called Lindsay Beckham the minute she sank into the chair behind her desk at Sharper Designs.

"Chassys bar."

"Is this Lindsay?"

"It is. Who's speaking?"

"Katie Winfield."

"Yes?"

"I did it."

"Did what?" the unflappable blonde asked. Even over the phone, she sounded cool and utterly in control.

"My Martini dare. You know, I made love in a forbidden place."

"Good for you." Was it her imagination or was there a self-satisfied note in Lindsay's voice? "And the object of your affections? What did he think about the dare?"

Katie grinned, thinking of the wiped-out expression on Liam's face. "I'm quite confident he liked it, too. Although I never told him that he was part of a dare."

"Excellent. As you know, you're sworn to secrecy about the details of your Martini dares. Are you ready for the next one?"

Katie sucked in her breath. Was she? Her encounter with Liam had been so intimately erotic she wasn't sure she was emotionally ready for another dare.

"You have to complete all three dares before next month's Martinis and Bikinis meeting," Lindsay reminded her.

"Yeah, okay, sure, send it my way."

"That's the spirit." Lindsay chuckled. "I'll put the new dare in the mail today."

"What was that all about?" Tanisha asked, after Katie had hung up.

"Um, nothing," she hedged.

"You've been acting very odd lately," Tanisha said. "Ever since Max made you art director. I think it's going to your head."

"It's not going to my head," she denied.

"No?" Tanisha looked as if she didn't believe it for a second.

"No."

"Well, something's wrong."

"Nothing's wrong."

"You—" she pointed a pitiless finger "—are seriously into denial."

Feeling badgered, she crossed her arms over her chest. "What makes you think something is wrong?"

"Because your skirt's on backward."

Katie looked down and saw that Tanisha was right. Her zipper was twisted around to the front, not in the back where it belonged. It must have happened in the theatre.

Her face heated. Good grief, she *was* seriously into denial.

Denial that her feelings for Liam were growing too fast and too strong.

Tanisha narrowed her eyes suspiciously. "Have you fallen off the cold-turkey wagon? Where were you during your lunch hour?"

Thankfully, her extension rang and she snatched up the receiver to avoid answering her friend's probing questions.

"Katie?"

She caught a skittish breath. The sound of Liam's voice, as spellbinding as snake-charmer music, curled through her body. Her tongue was cemented to the roof of her mouth and her hand tightened around the receiver. A dozen erotic images erupted in her mind.

She recalled the way he had looked at the movie theatre, muscles coiled tight, face scrunched up in ecstasy. Her hands tingled, recalling how her fingers had brushed against the smooth skin of his strong, clean-shaven jaw. Her nose twitched in memory of the tangy scent their lovemaking generated. Her mouth watered and her sex clenched with electric shivers. She wanted to do it again.

And soon.

But it wasn't just the physical act, and her enjoyment of it, that had her aching to be joined with him again. What she remembered most about their adventure in the theatre, what frayed her heart with an emotion she didn't want to think about, was the way he'd tenderly cupped her face in his hands. He'd stared deeply into her eyes and then kissed her lightly, tenderly, the moment after they'd climaxed together.

"Katie," he repeated.

"Uh-huh," she whispered, her pulse skipped a zealous message to her brain. *I want him.*

"I know this is short notice," he apologized, "but are you free on Wednesday night?"

"Um…what's up?"

"Mayor Delancy is having a dinner party at his house and I need a date. Can you come with me?"

Can I come with you? *That was a loaded question if she'd ever heard one.* "I'd love to."

"Great, I'll pick you up at seven-thirty." He rang off without another word.

Katie hung up, feeling a strange mix of emotions—anticipation mingled with sheepishness and a light dusting of bafflement. She'd been a flirt since childhood. Teasing men, leading them on and then taking off when things got too serious for her to handle. She liked keeping guys off balance, making them unsure of where they stood with her.

But Liam was different. Here he'd gone and asked her for a last-minute date and she hadn't hesitated. In the past—with any other guy—she would have pretended she had another date. Instead, she eagerly accepted Liam's invitation without thinking twice. How messed up was that?

Katie put a hand to her stomach, alarmed. Something very strange was happening to her. Something she could not control or explain.

And she wasn't at all sure she liked the path she was headed down.

9

LIAM PACED his penthouse apartment, his nerves shredded, even though he was loath to admit Finn Delancy held that much power over him. Tough guys didn't get nervous over being the guest of honor at dinner parties thrown by their illegitimate fathers.

The only thing that calmed him was the knowledge that he would have Katie by his side. She knew how to successfully navigate blue-blooded waters. One ally. That was all he needed to give him the strength to confront the man he'd never called father.

He picked Katie up in his Lamborghini at seven-thirty on the dot. She opened the door looking exactly like what she was—a well-bred Boston Brahmin. She wore a little black cocktail dress that fit her curves perfectly and showcased her sleek blond hair. The dress showed enough cleavage to be enticing without being vulgar. The skirt hem hit right above her knees. Not too long, not too short.

A five-carat diamond lay draped around her long slender neck, and she had on a matching bracelet. She'd twisted her hair up off her shoulders like Aubrey Hepburn in *Breakfast at Tiffany's*—his mother's all-time favorite movie.

She'd struck exactly the right note.

He stared, stunned by the simplicity of her beauty. "You look amazing."

Her smile was surprisingly shy. "Thank you."

"I brought you a corsage."

"I can see that."

He suddenly felt like a giant dork standing there with the vibrant red rose corsage in his hand. He'd gotten it on Vanessa's recommendation, but now the gesture seemed way too high-school-promish. "It's a dumb idea."

"No, no." She reached for the corsage. "Flowers are never a dumb idea."

"Should I pin it on for you?"

"Please."

He took the corsage out of the box and stepped forward to pin it on her dress. She smelled so good, so tempting. His knuckles grazed the curve of her skin, his fingertips brushing the velvety material of her dress. She felt so warm and alive.

Katie lowered her lashes, watching him pin the corsage in place. The fact she was watching him threw Liam off his game. Her succulent aroma, mingled with the smell of the roses, enticed him. He wanted to lean over and nibble on the creamy expanse of her exposed neck.

"Your thumb," she exclaimed. "Look, Liam, you're bleeding."

It was only then he noticed he had poked his finger with the pin while putting on her corsage. He'd been so overwhelmed by her that he hadn't even felt the prick of pain.

Katie snatched a tissue from a nearby box, reached out, took his hand and dotted away the blood.

Something knotted inside him at her tender touch. Something alien and scary.

He wondered how he looked to her, successful entrepreneur in a tux, Boston's most eligible bachelor, all suave and debonair, sticking his finger with a pin and not even paying attention because her beauty had so preoccupied him.

"Where did you get that tattoo?" she asked. "It doesn't fit with the rest of you."

He stiffened. He was sensitive about the tattoo. He wore wide watchbands to hide it, but when he looked down he could see the inky barbs peeping around the edge of his Rolex.

"I got into some trouble when I was a kid," he admitted, hoping a simple explanation would be enough.

"What kind of trouble?" She breathed, and he could tell she was intrigued.

"I got mixed up with a gang," he mumbled.

"A real gang?"

"Real enough."

She blinked. "I don't believe you."

He didn't know what possessed him to do what he did next. Her tone of voice, maybe. Or perhaps he had a desire to shock her. But the next thing Liam knew he was stripping off his jacket and unbuttoning his shirt.

A smile curled her lips. "I like the way this is going."

Her teasing frustrated him. He aimed to stun, not titillate.

He whipped off his shirt and then tugged down the

right side of his trouser waistband, revealing the jagged silvered scar just above his hipbone.

Katie's eyes widened to the size of quarters. "Ohmigod!"

Talking about being stabbed was more difficult than he'd thought it would be. But Liam was not prepared for what she did next.

Katie crossed the distance between them, sank to her knees and softly pressed her lips to his scar, leaving behind the scarlet imprint of her mouth branded against his skin. The gesture sent quivers shooting through his groin. Uncontrollably, his penis hardened. Disturbed by her response and his reaction to it, he held out a hand to help her to her feet.

"Tell me," she whispered, and touched his arm, leaving him wishing he'd never started this.

He lifted his shoulder, shrugging as if it had been no big deal, rather than a defining moment in his life. "It was the stupid mistake of a fourteen-year-old kid, looking for a place to belong."

"Why did you feel the need to belong that badly?"

"I grew up without a father. My mother worked two jobs to make ends meet. I spent a lot of time alone."

"What happened to your dad?"

He certainly hadn't intended on getting into all this now. "I never knew him. He took off the minute he found out my mother was pregnant."

"Wow, none of that was in the *Young Bostonian* article about you."

"I don't tell many people about it."

Her eyes softened. "Thank you for telling me."

"You're welcome."

"How did you get from there to where you are today?" She studied him intently, her gaze heating up his skin as he fumbled with the shirt buttons.

"After this—" he swept a hand at his scar "—my mother knew she had to get me out of that neighborhood or I was going to end up dead."

"How did she get you out of that environment?"

"She took a job as a cook's helper at a private school in upstate New York. Even though it paid a lot less than her two jobs in Boston, we were allowed to live in a two-room apartment on the school grounds and I received free tuition. If it weren't for the sacrifices she made, I wouldn't be here today."

That might sound overly dramatic, but it was the honest truth. He would have been killed or in prison, of that he had little doubt.

"How come you don't have the tattoo removed?"

"I keep it as a reminder of where I've been, of what I've escaped. I'm not proud of it, but it's important not to forget my past."

"Oh," she said as if she understood, but he knew she had no concept of what his life had been like. How could she from her ivory tower?

Looking at the regal tilt of her head, he felt like that fatherless fourteen-year-old boy again who'd grown up in the South Boston housing project. Unsure of himself and desperately longing for success, but terrified he'd never fit in with Katie's kind, no matter how hard he tried. He'd come a long way, but there were some barriers that could never be breached.

Who was he to think he could ever possess a woman

like her? He could amass all the money in the world and never be in her league. To believe otherwise was folly. His tattoo was proof of that. You couldn't change your DNA.

But part of his DNA was as blue-blooded as her own.

The part he hated.

Liam stepped back, hoping if he put some distance between them he could think more clearly, but he could not.

Katie met his gaze with a knowing smile. He had the frantic notion she could see right through him like an X-ray.

Afraid of his vulnerability, Liam cleared his throat. "We better leave if we don't want to be late for the mayor's party."

Delancy lived in one of the largest mansions on Beacon Hill. A valet hired for the evening parked his car. Liam took Katie's hand and guided her up the cobblestone walkway.

He noticed the carved lintels and decorative iron-work. Delancy was living here while he and his mother had been crammed into a six-hundred-square-foot apartment on the wrong side of the tracks and then later in an equally small garage apartment behind the dean's house at Fernwood Academy for Boys.

The old rage caught fire inside him.

Katie must have picked up on his mood because she stopped on the front doorstep and looked at him. "Liam, is everything okay?"

"Yes."

"You seem tense."

"A bit nervous, I guess."

"You?" She sounded surprised.

"I've never met the mayor before." At least not officially. Not outside of a pirate's costume.

"Don't be so impressed with Finn Delancy. My family's known his for years. People on Beacon Hill are like people anywhere else and most of them have a skeleton or two in their closet. Blue blood or not, you're twice the man Finn Delancy will ever be. Relax. You'll do fine."

Her words washed away his anger. She squeezed his hand, strengthening his courage and then reached out to rap the door with the heavy brass knocker.

A reserved-looking young woman wearing a starched white apron answered their knock.

"Liam James and Katie Winfield," Katie announced to the woman.

The mayor's home was something straight out of a nineteenth-century novel. The foyer towered two stories above their heads and the walls were paneled in luxurious mahogany. The rugs were Persian, the artwork original masterpieces and the massive chandelier looked as if it had come straight from the home of a Venetian artisan glassblower.

While my mother and I were eating macaroni and cheese, Delancy was living in a palace.

The woman took Katie's wrap and handbag and ushered them into the library where a group of Boston's elite were gathered around the fireplace sipping cocktails. The room was stocked floor to ceiling with books and overstuffed chairs. Liam would have killed to have access to such a library when he was in school.

"Katie, darling," a straw-thin, middle-aged woman

with a face smoothed by plastic surgery crossed the room to greet them. Liam recognized her from photos he'd seen in the newspaper and on TV as Delancy's wife, Sutton. "Don't tell me you've landed our city's most eligible multimillionaire bachelor."

"No, no," Katie said quickly. "Liam's a client of Sharper Design."

Her immediate denial that their relationship was anything more than business bothered him. Would it have been so terrible to let Sutton assume they were a couple?

Sutton linked her arm through Liam's, tugging him away from Katie. "You must tell me all about yourself, dear boy. You might be Boston's most eligible bachelor, but I've asked around and no one seems to know much about you other than the luscious fact that you're fabulously wealthy. Who is your family?"

He had to be careful. Much as he wanted to blurt out the truth, this wasn't the time or the place. He was here to get the lay of the land and to find out as much as he could about the enemy.

Finn Delancy broke away from his cronies at the fireplace and walked over to join Liam, Katie and Sutton in the middle of the room. He cradled a crystal tumbler of Scotch in his hand.

Liam didn't miss the lecherous look Finn sent in Katie's direction. He had to fight to suppress an overpowering urge to plant his fist in the older man's kisser.

"How do you do, Mr. James? I don't believe we've ever met." Delancy stuck out his hand.

Liam gritted his teeth. It was all he could do to civilly shake the man's hand. "No?"

Delancy looked confused by the questioning tone in Liam's voice.

Liam said nothing, just stared Delancy in the eyes. The mayor was the first to look away, shifting his attention to his glass of Scotch. "Can I get you something to drink?" Delancy searched the room for the maid, snapped his fingers at her and said, "Alice, get Mr. James a…"

"Whiskey," Liam said. He wasn't much for hard liquor, but this evening was shaping up to be a whiskey kind of night. "Neat."

Delancy reached up and put a hand on Liam's shoulder. "Come on over and let me introduce you to everyone."

He flinched at the intimate contact, turned his head to look for Katie and found her right beside him. If not for her, he would feel like a hapless sheep among a pack of wolves. He might know how to make money and flip real estate, but he didn't have a clue how to walk the delicate tightrope of high-society politics.

Everyone at the party knew Katie and while Liam had met a few of the people in the room at various functions, he knew none of them personally. He chatted with State Senator Gerard Clarkson and his wife, Nancy, along with two CEOs of Boston's largest corporations, a retired PGA superstar and their dates.

Alice brought Liam his whiskey and he took a bracing swallow. Katie was charming the crowd, regaling them with stories of her family, taking the pressure off him. He ended up in one corner, shoulder propped against the wall, watching her dazzle the guests. She would make someone a wonderful wife someday.

The thought sent a fissure of jealousy through him. He didn't want to think of her as someone else's wife.

Occasionally she paused in the middle of her conversation to cast a sidelong glance his way. There was no question about it—Katie captivated him.

She also scared him.

"Dinner is served," Alice announced from the doorway.

Everyone trooped into the large dining room. The table was lavishly but very tastefully set with expensive but simple patterned china, genuine silverware and crystal goblets. A roasted goose was the main attraction.

Liam started to sit next to Katie, but Sutton Delancy intervened. "No, no, we don't sit with our dates."

Her chastisement over his faux pas sent a heated rush of embarrassment through Liam, reminding him how out of place he was here.

He remembered something he'd read once. When riding in a car, lower-class couples sit beside their spouses, middle-class couples sit with men in the front seat and women in the back, and the ruling classes sit with each other's spouses.

And here he was, uncomfortable with the ruling class. He looked over at Katie, who seemed totally at ease.

"You're the guest of honor," Sutton went on. "You must take your place here, young man." She pulled out the chair at the head of the table.

Delancy took the spot directly opposite Liam at the foot of the table and guided Katie to sit at his right hand. Sutton sat to Liam's left as the remainder of the guests found their places.

"So tell us," Sutton began, after the maid served the

first course of bouillabaisse, "how did you get started in real estate? The way you're going, you'll own half of Boston within the next five years."

Liam shifted, uncomfortable in the hot seat. "I fixed up my first car when I was a kid, sold it for double what I paid for it. Did that enough times until I could afford to by a small house and I renovated it. Then I flipped it, reinvested the money in a new house and the rest is history."

"Goodness," said Nancy Clarkson, fanning herself. "He's wealthy, handsome, passionate and hardworking. Hang on to this one, Katie. He's a keeper."

"Your initiative is impressive," Delancy said.

Liam glared down the end of the table. He contemplated blurting out the mayor's dirty secret right then and there, and he took perverse delight in imagining the shocked reactions.

But then his gaze caught Katie's. The last thing he wanted was to look like anything less than a hero in her eyes. The realization bothered him, but it was the truth.

"I read in the *Young Bostonian* article that you grew up in a South Boston housing project," Delancy said.

The hairs on his forearms lifted. He drilled his gaze into the mayor's, holding on tight to his anger. "That's right."

Katie was watching.

"You'd be the perfect person to introduce me at this year's ribbon-cutting ceremony for my Habitat for Humanity project," Delancy continued. "Local gang-banger not only turns good but becomes a multimillionaire in the process."

Rage tinged with degradation froze Liam's blood. He

curled his fingers around the silver spoon in his hand. Could Delancy have figured out who he was? Could that be the real reason he'd been invited here tonight?

"Has a certain cachet, don't you think?"

Liam forced a slow smile, smacking his gaze hard against Delancy's, giving the mayor a menacing, predatory stare. "How do you know I was in a gang?"

Delancy's returning smile was uncertain. "Why, Katie told me a few minutes ago."

Liam swung his stare around to capture Katie with it. Nervously, she licked her lips. "I...didn't know your past was a secret."

Her betrayal of his confidence wounded like a razor's blade. He bit down the inside of his cheek, mentally berating himself for having trusted her.

"I'm sorry," she murmured, but had the strength of courage to hold his gaze.

He realized then he'd been looking at her the same way he'd been looking at Delancy. As if she were the enemy. Her blue eyes pleaded with him for forgiveness. God, how could he hold a grudge when she looked so remorseful and beautiful?

Liam shrugged, softened his gaze. "It wasn't a secret," he said. "I've got nothing to hide."

"Then you'll introduce me at the Habitat for Humanity ceremony?" Delancy prodded.

Liam kept his eyes on Katie. It was the only way he could hold his contempt for the man in check. "All right."

What was it about Katie Winfield that twisted his insides into knots? Just the act of tracking the snowy skin between her pear-studded earlobes and slender collarbone made Liam forget everything except pressing his lips to that vulnerable spot.

"It's settled, then." Delancy dusted his palms together. "The ribbon-cutting ceremony is on the twentieth at noon. Make sure to mark your calendar."

"I won't forget." Liam looked back at Delancy, silently acknowledging that he'd just agreed to do a favor for the creep. Tension locked his neck muscles. But then it occurred to him that the ceremony—complete with media coverage—was the prime opportunity and the perfect venue to exact his revenge upon Delancy.

The maid reappeared to clear the soup bowls and to ask if anyone needed fresh drinks.

"Could I have another whiskey, please?" Liam asked. It was the only way he was going to make it through this damnable dinner.

Katie, Liam noted, missed nothing. He could see it in her eyes and the way she held herself with a calm stillness. She might be young, but in some ways she was much more worldly than him.

She put a smile on her face and lavishly praised the Caesar salad that was served as their second course.

By the end of the meal, Katie had managed to defuse any tension running through the room, although there was still plenty of tension coursing inside Liam that even two tumblers of the finest whiskey in the world could not stop.

"It was so interesting to meet you," Sutton said as she ushered her guests toward the front door. She took Liam's hand in hers and squeezed it. "I'm so looking forward to the Habitat for Humanity ceremony."

After a round of goodbyes with everyone who was

still there, Katie took Liam firmly by the elbow and escorted him out the front door. The valet brought his car around and handed Liam the keys.

But as he reached for the door, Katie closed her hand around his.

"Give me your keys," she demanded, and held out her palm. "You've had too much to drink and I'm driving you home."

"You could take me back to your place and have your way with me." He winked.

She wrinkled her nose. "Given the circumstances, I'll pass. Keys, please."

"Have you ever driven a Lamborghini?"

"No, but it can't be that hard."

He didn't want to give up control, but the determined set to her chin told him she was right. He shouldn't be driving. Not so much from the whiskey, but more from the distracted edginess lingering inside him. The last thing the streets of Boston needed was one more case of road rage.

"This point is nonnegotiable." She looked him in the face, a combination of concern, disappointment and resolve written in the depths of her blue eyes. "Give me your keys, Liam, or I'm calling the cops."

He laughed at her. She looked so fierce.

"I'm not kidding."

"When you put it like that, what choice do I have?"

"Precisely."

"Okay," he agreed. "But let this serve as a warning. You wreck my car and you'll live to regret it, Winfield," he said before handing over his car keys and opening the driver-side door for her.

10

KATIE'S FOREARM burned from the brush of Liam's knuckles as he closed the car door. Her breath hung as she watched him hurry around to the passenger side and then climb in beside her. It took him a couple of seconds of fumbling before he had his seat belt locked securely in place.

She stuck the key in the ignition and the Lamborghini's powerful engine rumbled to life. The leather seats wrapped around her. She reached over and snapped on the radio. Classical music poured from the stereo speakers. Mozart, she recognized. One of his more gallopy tunes.

"It's a manual," Liam said. "Six-speed. You know how to handle a stick?"

She lowered her lashes, slanted him a surreptitious look. "I know my way around a gearshift."

A whiskey-laced smile languidly curled his lips. "What about a five-hundred-horsepower, ten-cylinder big block engine? Know how to handle one of those?"

"You tell me after the ride."

"You know these babies go from zero to sixty in four seconds."

Katie licked her lips. "That's a lot of thrust."

"It is."

"Impressive," she said. "But there is something to be said for a more leisurely ascent."

"Top speed is a hundred-and-ninety-two miles an hour." She could hear the smile in his tone.

"You've been holding out on me, James."

"How's that?"

"Pretending that you're staid Mister Workaholic without an adventuresome bone in his body, but then you're driving a work of art like this." She patted the leather dashboard. "There's danger lurking in your soul. You've been covering it up."

"You think so?"

"I know so, and I intend on rocking your world."

"You already have," he said. "So don't rock my car."

She laughed and put the Lamborghini in Drive. Her nipples tightened, part excitement, part fear. She was glad he could only see her profile, glad the night was dark. But even as she told herself this, she couldn't help turning her head for a better look at him.

His shoulders were angled toward her, his gaze beaded on her. The glow from the dashboard light threw shadows over his angular jaw. His scent heightened her awareness. Expensive whiskey, combined with woodsy cologne and the rich smell of leather. Her father used to have a similar fragrance—manly, grounded, trustworthy.

Liam was looking at her with a kind of wonder.

In the dimness, his face appeared craggier, more rugged than in light. His thick dark hair stood up slightly in the back, an errant lock refusing to stay down. The look in his eyes changed. And along with it the intensity of the tugging sensation in her belly increased. There was a flicker of something golden in his eyes, something wild and unexpected.

The form of his lips changed, his posture, the slant of his eyebrows. He was someone else entirely. Bachelor of the year no more, this man was darker. He'd seen things, dark things. She thought of his childhood brush with street gangs and her heart tweaked.

Katie was thankful for the console that kept their thighs from touching. Otherwise, she doubted she could have kept all four tires on the road.

Her fingers gripped the smooth ball of the gearshift head and slipped it into the next gear as they left the driveway and merged onto the street.

LIAM SAT beside Katie, his pulse pumping faster than the Lamborghini's heated pistons. He didn't like being in the passenger seat at the mercy of her driving skills, out of control of his own vehicle. He wished he could edge her aside and slip behind the wheel, but she was right. He'd had too much to drink and his reaction time wasn't what it should be.

Neither were his cognitive skills, because he found himself thinking thoughts that were better left suppressed. Enticing, dangerous thoughts about what it would feel like to ride in the car beside her every day for the rest of his life.

"You wanna see how I handle big boys' toys?" She challenged and, without waiting for his reply, hit the freeway doing seventy.

She tossed her head like a high-spirited filly. Her hair fell forward, the tips of the light blond strands grazing the top of her cleavage. She reached up to slide a lock of hair behind one pearl-studded ear.

Liam felt the rhythm of her movements rush straight through his stomach and into his groin. Something about the way she handled the quivering thrust of his V10 engine inflamed him. She was like a luxury sports car herself, with fine rounded curves and bosoms protruding like headlights.

Enveloped in their cocoon of precision machinery, she rushed him through time and space. Speed, wrapped inextricably with sexual need, gushed through his brain, his limbs and his entire body. She was fast and adventuresome and exciting. And he worshipped her in an orgy of pure velocity.

Liam was so busy filling up with testosterone that her next comment took him by surprise.

"You want to tell me what happened back there with the mayor?" Katie asked. "Or are you just going to let me believe you're a total horse's ass?"

"You picked up on that?"

Katie grinned. "Give me some credit, will you? A blind woman could have picked up on your animosity toward Delancy. Thing is, I get the distinct impression he has no idea that you hate him."

"You're very perceptive."

"Don't sound so amazed. Just because I like to keep to the lighter side of things doesn't mean I'm clueless."

"I never said you were clueless."

"You thought it."

"Never. Impetuous yes, clueless never," he admitted.

"I also noticed that you didn't answer my question," she prodded.

"Which question was that?"

"Why do you hate Finn Delancy?"

"It's complicated."

"Guyspeak for you don't want to talk about it."

"Yeah."

"Why not?"

"Why not what?"

She cocked her head and gave him a piercing glance before returning her attention to the road. "Why don't you want to talk about it?"

"Because it's none of your business."

"It might not be any of my business, but you certainly look like you need to talk about it."

"I don't need to talk about it."

"How long have you kept this—" she waved a hand "—complicated thing bottled up?"

"All my life," he said, and then immediately regretted it.

"You've got a dark secret."

"Not really. Just something I'm not particularly proud of."

"You might feel better if you got it off your chest," she ventured.

"I seriously doubt it."

"The thing about secrets is," she went on, ignoring his denial that he had a secret, "once you tell someone about them, they no longer hold any power over your life."

"I don't have any secrets. In fact," he said, "I hate secrets and dishonest people."

"So is Delancy the dishonest person with the secret?" she guessed. "Do you have something on him?"

"Sort of."

"And you don't approve of him."

"I hate him."

"If you dislike the man so much, how come you accepted his dinner invitation? How come you agreed to introduce him at the Habitat for Humanity event?"

"Can we not talk about Delancy?"

"Okay." She surprised him by suddenly letting go of the conversation.

Silence fell. All they could hear were engine sounds and road noises.

From the time his mother had told him his father's identity when he was sixteen, Liam had plotted and schemed and planned for his success. He'd studied hard in school, played every sport Fernwood Academy offered and did lots of volunteer work. He got straight A's and won a merit scholarship to Harvard. He cut clippings of his achievements and made scrapbooks. He'd graduated cum laude from Harvard Business School, all the while buying run-down houses in South Boston and restoring them for resale.

Because of his achievements, women were crazy for him. And other than his glorious mistake with Arianna, there hadn't been room in his life for romance. He'd had a few girlfriends, yes. But somehow he'd managed to always keep things casual. It was easier that way. Nobody got hurt.

The truth was, he secretly longed for a family of his own while at the same time he feared it. What did he know about being a good father? He'd certainly had no role models. And what if he couldn't stop his work-aholic pace? His work had always defined him. If he wasn't driven to succeed, then who was he?

And Liam had been keeping his relationships super-ficial for so long, he realized he didn't know how to take things deeper with a woman. He didn't know how to let go of his work and enjoy his life, mainly, because real estate *was* his life.

Liam watched her downshift around a corner. She almost ran a red light, the yellow slipping to crimson just as she made it through the intersection.

"Yellow means slow down, not go faster," he said.

"Not in a Lamborghini it doesn't." She grinned wickedly.

His heart chugged. "You're one sexy woman, Katie Winfield."

"Oh, don't start. You're drunk and I'm pissed off at you for not trusting me with your dark secret."

"I'm not that drunk." He reached over to lightly fin-ger a strand of hair curling at her shoulder. "And you're not that pissed off."

"I am," she asserted.

"What will it take to get you unpissed?"

"Tell me what's going on inside that head of yours. What's your beef with Finn Delancy?"

Liam cocked his head and studied her for a long mo-ment. *Confess.* Maybe this was what he needed to do in order to take things to a new level with her. "You really want to hear the whole sordid story?"

She nodded. "I do."

"Promise you won't pity me?"

"I promise."

He took a deep breath. "Pull over."

"I'm not letting you behind the wheel."

"I don't want to drive, just find a place to pull over. I need to get out and walk."

"Are you sick?"

"I'm not sick. I just…I've never told this story to anyone and I need to get out of the car, clear my head, make sure I want to do this."

She obeyed his command, slowing down, driving through a residential neighborhood until she found a community park. She pulled into the vacant lot near some swings and parked beneath a maple tree near a streetlamp. She cut the engine and leaned back in the seat.

"Let's walk," he said.

They got out. The air was nippy, but not uncomfortably so. He headed for the jogging trail, Katie at his side. They walked for several minutes without speaking.

"I'm a bastard." Liam found himself saying in a calm, unemotional voice.

Katie clicked her tongue in sympathy. "Don't be so hard on yourself. So you had a little too much to drink and looked a bit sketchy in front of the mayor and his guests. Don't worry about it."

"No, I'm a bastard. For real." He laughed harshly. "Although some people might argue I'm the other kind of bastard, as well."

"You're saying your mother wasn't married to your father when you were born?"

"That's right."

"Big deal."

"Big deal?"

"I read something like thirty percent of children are born out of wedlock these days. No one cares."

"Spoken like someone who grew up in a loving, nuclear family."

"Hey, my life hasn't been a bed of roses. My father was strict military and a prominent member of Boston society. You have no idea the expectations that entails. Plus, I've lost both my parents within the past five years. Everyone has their cross to bear, Liam."

KATIE BURROWED deeper into her coat and scurried to keep up with his long-legged stride. Liam had increased the pace. In the distance a dog barked and a porch light went on. He was clearly ambivalent about this subject. "You don't have to tell me any more about it, Liam. Forget it. I don't want to be the cause of you having to have therapy."

"No, no." He stopped walking and made an about-face to stare at her. "I want to tell you."

"So tell me. I'm listening."

He heaved in a breath. "Okay, my mother came to Boston from Ireland when she was only seventeen. A friend got her a job working in a factory that made parts for sailing ships. The owner of the factory was a Beacon Hill Brahmin with eyes for my mother. She didn't know he was married when they started dating. He wined her, dined her, treated her like royalty. Told her the kind of lies that make a young girl's heart light up. Then when she found out she was pregnant with his child, he threw three hundred dollars at her and told her to get an abortion."

"It must have been awful for your mom."

Liam was breathing hard. He had his fists clenched. The muscles in his neck were bunched so tightly Katie could feel his anger. "Yeah."

She touched his arm. "And for you, too."

He didn't say anything for so long that she finally prompted, "So what did your mother do after that?"

"There wasn't anywhere she could stay. There was a home for unwed mothers in Boston, but you had to give your child up for adoption if you stayed there. She refused to give me up. I was all she had. She'd lost all her family in Ireland. That's why she'd come to America."

"How did she get through it?"

"She had two jobs, worked in a different factory at night, pressed clothes in a dry-cleaning shop by day. Hard, backbreaking work, but the owners of the dry cleaner's allowed her to bring me to work with her after I was born. On weekends, she took classes and earned both her U.S. citizenship and her GED. She raised me all on her own without one penny of assistance from my so-called father."

Katie's heart hurt. For Liam, for his mother, for the struggles they must have endured. "I think I understand you," she said.

He stared at her with his sharp, intelligent eyes. The look unsettled her. "Have I scared you off because I'm so damaged?"

Katie raised her chin. "Everyone's damaged in one way or an other. Besides, I don't scare easily."

He nodded, but he shrugged as if he didn't believe her. Suddenly, she didn't believe what she'd said, either.

Every impulse in her body was urging her to kiss him, but she didn't want him to misunderstand it. Hell, she didn't want to misunderstand it. She felt something for this man. Something too powerful to take lightly. He could hurt her. She could hurt him. They could hurt each other very badly if they weren't very careful.

"I haven't told you the biggest secret yet."

"I'm listening."

"Finn Delancy?"

"Yes?"

"You want to know why I hate him?"

She nodded, but she already knew what he was going to say. He merely confirmed it.

"He's the guy. He's my father."

Katie concentrated on his features. It explained a lot, and now that he mentioned it, she could see a bit of physical resemblance between the two men. "But he doesn't know who you are."

He gave a harsh laugh. "No."

"You resent people born into wealth and prominence, don't you?"

He stuffed his hands in his pockets. "Not admirable, but it's the truth."

Once he admitted it, a bleakness fell over her. He was with her because of her pedigree, who she was. That's why he'd invited her to the dinner party, in effect, flaunt-ing her. Making this subliminal statement: *Hey, look*

*at me. I'm from the streets and I've nailed me a
woman who can trace her family tree back to the May-
flower.*

Wretchedly, she closed her eyes, then opened them
again to find him focused on her.

"What's wrong?"

"You're using me."

"What?"

"You're using me to get what has always been out of
your reach, no matter how hard you've worked. I'm
your entrée into Boston society. You made the money
on your own, but you can't buy a pedigree."

"No," he vehemently denied. "I'm not."

She was feeling sick to her stomach. "Really? First
you date Brooke and when there is no love connection
between the two of you, then you come after me." She
turned and walked back to the Lamborghini, but he
caught her by the arm and spun her around to face him.

"That's unfair. You seduced me at the Ladies
League Ball."

"You expect me to believe my last name doesn't have
anything to do with why I'm here with you?"

"Okay," he said. "Maybe Brooke's heritage was
the reason I was initially attracted to her, but the minute I met you, all bets were off. You…me—" He
pointed from her to him and back again. "This thing
between us has nothing to do with our social standing
or our past."

"I wish I could believe you," she said, not knowing
what to think, unable to decipher what she was feeling.

He tilted her chin, forcing her to look up at him. "I

won't ever lie to you, Katie. All I ask in return is that you never lie to me."

"If I was dead broke and named Katie Smith, you'd still be here with me."

"Damn straight."

LIAM WAS ALARMED to think she could believe he was using her for his own gain. He had to show Katie how much she meant to him. He pulled her to him, slid his hands up the back of her neck to cup her head in his palms.

Her hair was a soft and silky slide beneath his fingers. And the rhythmic rise and fall of her chest sent his own breath reeling. A heated awareness pricked his skin. Their mental connection was undeniable. He'd never felt so conscious of anything in his life.

She looked at him, her eyes shining bright and eager in the glow of light from the overhead vapor lamp. She made him feel unique, and yet he had no right to feel that way. Katie was an adventurous woman, no doubt about it. From her mischievous grin, to her rakish smile, she appreciated sex.

And no woman had ever aroused him so intently.

She was playful and flirtatious and spontaneous; he was reserved and sober and scrupulous. She was windblown; he walked the straight and narrow. She lived to shock; he kept his feelings to himself. She was a blue blood and he'd been born with a plastic fork in his mouth. She was foie gras; he was a TV dinner.

And he was falling for her hard and fast.

Falling so hard and so fast that he didn't even notice where they were.

You're just horny, he told himself but Liam was afraid that wasn't the whole truth. He was terrified he was starting to care more for her than she could ever care for him.

She pursed her lips.

He kissed her then, every cell in his body humming in harmony with hers.

She kissed him back, increasing the pressure, upping the tempo. Her lips blasted him into another realm of awareness, making him forget everything except the feel of her mouth under his. Her short fingernails dug into the back of his head. A deep flush of arousal painted her face, spread down her neck to her perky bosom. She was ready for action.

The flick of her tongue over his teeth was lazy, sultry, teasing him by degrees. Slowly at first, but then with steadily building pressure.

Liam didn't remember how, but they made it back to the car. He wasn't thinking, just reacting—blindly, crazily—and was mad to have her again and again and again.

They stood beside the Lamborghini, Katie's back against the passenger side. Liam pressed against her.

His head spun, his heart pounded. His hand slipped down to cup her tight, round bottom. His penis strained against his zipper. Flexing, he curled his fingers into the soft, willing flesh of her buttocks. He heard her quick intake of breath, and it ignited him.

"Now," she said. "I need you. Now."

Then she reached up under the hem of her sexy black dress, pulled down her panties and stepped out of them. With her index finger, she made a slingshot of her red thong and shot it through the air. The tiny scrap of silk sailed over his shoulder.

Agog, Liam stared hard as she bent over the back of the Lamborghini, waggled her sweet little ass in the air and whispered, "Come and get me."

11

THE SOUND of his zipper sliding down was incredibly erotic in the still of the chilly, dark night. The crinkling of a condom being opened caused her womb to contract. The feel of the cool, metal curve of the Lamborghini against her belly served to spike her desire even higher. The spicy taste of anticipation filled her mouth. Katie's heart fluttered.

But the smooth glide of his hot, palm sliding up the hem of her skirt to cup her bare ass was Katie's undoing.

Liam bent over her, pressed his lips to her ear and whispered, "Wild thing."

She swallowed desperately, felt his erect penis throbbing through the folds of his pants. He pressed himself against her butt. She felt his body swell harder still. Combing aside her hair, he dipped his head and lightly nipped the nape of her neck with his teeth.

The hot wetness of his lips ignited her and the waves of passion that had been rising inside her streamed molten.

With both his hands now up under her dress and splayed across her bottom, he cocked his knee up and used it to spread her legs farther apart.

His hands slipped from her bottom up to her waist,

his wrists pushing up the skirt of her dress in the process. The cool air on her naked skin drove goose bumps up her spine.

Groaning, he rocked against her. "Beautiful, so damned beautiful."

She whimpered as the deep center of her feminine core constricted and her nipples squeezed down to rock-hard pebbles beneath the silk of her bra.

He reached up to weave the fingers of one hand through her hair at the same time he ground his hips against hers. Holding her firmly in place, he ran his devilish tongue down the back of her neck.

It was totally erotic, sandwiched between Liam's hot body and the cool metal of one of the world's most expensive automobiles. Shivering, she flexed her inner muscles, desperate to drive as hard as this precision sports car.

They were in the open park, hidden only by midnight and a privacy hedge shielding them from direct view of the neighborhood development behind them. At any moment a car could drive by and expose them.

The thrill of the notion stole her breath.

Liam's fingers tightened in her hair, pulling her head up as if she were an untamed mare and he her wild stallion.

"Tell me you want me."

"I want you," she panted. "I want you inside of me now!"

Then he was in her, and she gasped at the immediate insurgence of pure pleasure. He filled her up so completely she might not be able to take any more.

"You're so wet, babe," he murmured. "Dripping wet for me."

"All for you."

He felt so good. Hard, lean, and strong. Her hips twitched against his, the muscles between her thighs clenching tight.

Their breathing pattern altered, grew more ragged, more urgent. Their mating was primal. Ferocious. He plunged heedlessly into her. Driving them closer and closer to the edge.

The stars twinkled overhead. The wind rustled against their fevered skin.

"Harder," she cried. "Faster."

Liam's cock pounded, sending her spiraling upward, higher and higher. Her ears rang. Flashes of heat rolled through her. The feel of his big body behind her, his thick fingers fanned out over her ass, flung her into the stratosphere.

And when she believed she absolutely could not take any more pleasure, he separated her aching cheeks with a palm. His thumb pressed gently against the pucker of her bottom causing a sizzling jolt of white-hot lightning to shoot through her nerve endings.

Katie lost her last shred of control. She'd never felt anything so exquisite. She screamed his name and her spine arched at the piercing intensity of the sensation.

Liam was equally crazed. He slammed relentlessly into her. His cock was a sword and she the waiting scabbard. He moved his hips and his hand in unison, satisfying her sex with his, caressing her in a secret place she'd never been caressed before. Supplying her with new dreams to dream, fresh fantasies.

Glorious.

She gasped.

Her womb spasmed, squeezing him tight as her muscles clenched around his exploring thumb.

"You like that?"

"More," she pleaded. "More."

"My pleasure."

Amidst the sultry haze, inside the warmth of her own skin, Katie closed her eyes and breathed in the power of the moment, experiencing everything—the distinct contrast between the soft velvet of her dress, the hard metal of the car and the friction of Liam's skin.

This was a memory she planned to treasure forever. She memorized the deep bass thud of her heart; experienced the taste of her desire, sharp and sweet as strawberries; savored the thick ebb and flow of blood rolling through her arms and legs. And, she accepted the uncertain sureness of fear breathing into her ear. *Don't enjoy this too much. It's only temporary. It's nothing but a dare.*

He drove into her one more time and she was gone.

Katie felt weighted in a deliciously lazy way, as if she were floating, hanging, flying high. Her thoughts retreated. Her mind emptied as her body filled up, dragging away her ability to form full sentences. Words slipping through her head like beads on a pearl necklace.

She. He. The Lamborghini. The luxurious night.

Heat. Flesh. Bodies. Thumbs.

Adventure. Excitement. Lust. Love.

Love?

No, no, not love.

Maybe not love, but sincere like and lots and lots and lots of lust.

There was no escaping the power of their lust for each other. He'd captured her, made her his prisoner, and taken her free will. She was nothing but his sex slave and she loved her sentence.

It took her down.

The orgasm. Splendid and brilliant as a shooting star.

The power took her down. Down, down, down. Into a place she'd never before explored.

She heard Liam cry out. Moments later, he was pulling her up, turning her around and tugging her into the crook of his arm. They clung to each other, their bodies glued with perspiration and honeyed sex.

His fingers stroked her hair, pushing it out of her eyes. She looked at him, searched his face for any signs that what he'd felt was just as monumental as what she'd experienced. Afraid to see the answer, terrified equally of either yes or no.

He smiled softly, dipped his head, captured her lips and kissed away her doubt. He'd taken this as she'd intended. Living in the moment, enjoying himself.

Katie breathed in the scent of him, along with a sigh of relief, but she couldn't figure out why she suddenly felt so impossibly sad.

DREAMILY, Katie gazed out her office window, her mind on Liam. No matter how hard she tried to focus on the art graphics design for his ad campaign, she couldn't stop thinking about him.

Or the rather wanton way she'd acted.

Katie cringed. What was the matter with her? Why did she possess this constant need to outdo herself by finding ways to shock and surprise him? The sex had been mindblowing, but she couldn't help feeling bitter-sweet about it. Their relationship was based on nothing more than a silly dare.

And speaking of dares, the latest one had arrived in her mailbox that morning. She'd stuffed it in her purse on her way to work, and there it sat, unopened.

Mocking her.

She glanced under her desk at her purse. She could see the corner of pink linen paper peeking out at her. Part of her couldn't wait to rip it open and discover what exciting Martini dare awaited inside that gilded envelope. But another part of her was scared of what the dare might say.

You don't have to do it, you know. Just toss it in the trash, forget all about the Martini dare.

But Katie had never been one to walk away from a challenge. She pulled the envelope from her purse and leaned it against her coffee mug. Propping her elbows on the desk, she sank her chin into her upturned palms and glowered at the envelope.

It might sound like a romantic cliché, but she'd never met a man like Liam. When she thought of him, her heart grew full and achy and her stomach twisted up in knots.

She remembered the innocent things about him. The way his unexpected smile made her light up inside, the reassuring sound of his rich comforting voice, the spark of passion in his eyes when he looked at her.

And no man had ever responded to her sexual teasing in quite the same way that he did. Magically, he hard-ened at the slightest brush of her hand. Provocatively, he took the bait when she challenged him to expand his sexual horizons. Bravely, he followed where she led, and yet he made it seem as if he were the one doing the leading.

His sense of adventure matched hers—even if he was just now discovering it. The power of his life force was a thing of awe. He was secure in his masculinity and self-confident in business. And he made her feel like the sexiest woman on Earth.

She thought about the secret he'd told her—that he was the illegitimate son of Finn Delancy. She tried to imagine what that felt like—growing up without a father, never feeling that he was good enough, having to find his own way in the world.

It explained so much about him and made her love him all the more.

Love?

No, no, she didn't mean *love*. She admired him, yes. But that was all. *Love* was much too strong of a word. Love required too much of her. Most definitely, this feeling wasn't the budding bloom of love. Maybe it was time she cut the relationship short before things got too complicated.

She thought of how terrific sex was with him. How good she felt when they were together. How simply looking at him or thinking about him made her pulse quicken and palms grow damp.

Her gaze fell on the envelope.

Well, maybe one more date.

She reached for the dare, opened it and read.

You are hereby dared to have sex in an exotic place.

Exotic place? Hmm.

She thought of the bungalow her family owned in Fiji. How easy it was to think of her and Liam walking the white sand beaches, sipping festive umbrella drinks, feeling the balmy tropical breezes on their skin. Not to mention making love in a hammock under a bright starry sky.

Goose bumps scattered up her arm. Erotic and exotic.

But how to get Liam to go to Fiji?

Before she could formulate a plan of action, the sound of Tanisha dragging into the office twenty minutes late drew Katie's attention to her coworker.

She took in Tanisha's disheveled appearance, wrinkled clothes, her lovely braids coming undone, eyes red-rimmed. She'd never seen her confident, stylish friend looking so demolished.

Katie sprang to her side. "Omigosh, are you all right?"

"No," Tanisha whimpered, and plopped down in her chair, knees pressed together, feet splayed apart.

Katie knelt beside her, wrapped her hand around Tanisha's forearm. "What is it?"

"It's Dwayne."

"Has something happened to him?"

"He broke up with me." Tanisha's voice cracked, and a single tear slid down her caramel cheek.

That solitary heartbreaking tear startled Katie. She'd never seen her friend cry, much less shed a tear over some guy. She pulled a tissue from the box on the desk and pressed it into Tanisha's hand. "Oh, honey, I'm so sorry. What happened?"

"He said he couldn't trust me." Tanisha pressed the tissue to her eye.

"Why would he say that?"

"Because," Tanisha mumbled, "I sort of lied to him."

"Sort of?"

"He wanted to be open and honest. He told me about his past, the women he'd known, and then he wanted to know how many men I'd been with."

"What'd you tell him?"

"Two." Tanisha cringed.

"Why did you lie?"

"Because he'd only been with two women. How could I tell him the truth? I was afraid he would think I was slutty or something."

"So how'd he find out that you weren't being honest with him?"

"He met Jerome."

"Your brother ratted you out?"

Tanisha nodded, sniffled. "He said if I would lie to him about this kind of thing, how could he trust me when it came to the important stuff?"

"You were only trying to salvage his ego."

"I know," Tanisha wailed.

"He placed you in a no-win situation."

"Exactly, but he's an honesty-is-the-best-policy type of guy."

Katie let out a soft sigh. It certainly didn't sound like a happily-ever-after ending for her friend. To think, strong-minded, independent Tanisha was reduced to rubble over a man. If it could happen to her, it could happen to anyone. Her heart gave a strange jerk of disappointment and she realized she'd secretly been rooting for Tanisha's relationship with Dwayne to be of the soul-mate variety.

See what happens when you believe in fairy tales?

Katie rose to her feet. This was precisely why she avoided committed relationships—too much chance for heartache.

"I knew better than to tell Dwayne a white lie. I made a mistake. I know it now. But he won't even take my calls."

Not knowing what else to do, Katie patted her friend's shoulder. "I'm so sorry you're hurting."

"You were right to stick to sex and avoid romantic entanglements," Tanisha said. "Love, marriage, happily-ever-after, it's all bullshit."

"No." Katie shook her head. "I was wrong. Yes, maybe I've never been hurt, but I've also never had the depth of intimacy you found with Dwayne."

But you could have it, if you let yourself.

Yeah, right, willingly lay herself open to the kind of pain Tanisha was suffering. No thank you.

"I love him so much. I've never felt this way before and it's ripping me apart inside to think I've lost him because of my own stupidity. How can I ask him to forgive me when he won't even talk to me?"

"If he's this unforgiving, maybe he's not the right one for you," Katie ventured.

"He was the one," Tanisha said, and shed another tear.

"Then if Dwayne's the one, you guys will work this out," Katie said, not believing what she was saying but knowing it was the only thing that would make Tanisha feel better.

"You really think so?"

Katie crossed her fingers behind her back, telling her own white lie. "Absolutely. Give him some time to deal with his bruised ego and he'll figure out he can't live without you."

Tanisha smiled sadly through the tears. "Thank you, Katie, for being such a good friend. You're probably right, the male ego being what it is. Dwayne really is a stand-up guy."

Katie forced a smile of her own. For Tanisha's sake, she prayed it was true.

WHILE KATIE was consoling Tanisha, Liam was staring out the big plate-glass window of his office building watching the bustling city go about its daily activity. He knew she was holding back, keeping her emotions in check. Using sex to keep from experiencing something deeper. He had a feeling she'd been using adventure as a barrier against intimacy for most of her life. He'd just had to figure out a way to knock that wall down.

Truth was, he was out of his league when it came to this romantic stuff. But like any successful executive, he knew where to turn to find answers. Breezing past Vanessa, he headed down the corridor to Tony's office.

He knocked at Tony's door but charged in without waiting to be invited.

Tony glanced up from his paperwork. "Hey, boss, what's up?"

"I need your advice."

"Sure." Tony tossed down his pen, leaned back in his chair. "What can I do for you?"

This suddenly seemed like a stupid idea, and Liam almost turned on his heel and walked away. But the thought of winning Katie's heart had him taking a seat across from his best friend's desk.

"I'm here for you. What do you need to say?" Tony arched his eyebrows.

"It's complicated."

Tony steepled his fingers. "Do you want my advice or not."

Liam cleared his throat. "Okay, here's the deal, I think I'm falling in love with Katie, but she's terrified of intimacy and I don't know how to get through to her."

Tony snorted. "Katie's not the only one afraid of intimacy."

"What's that supposed to mean?"

"How many years has your love life taken a backseat to romance?"

"Thirty-one," Liam admitted.

"Exactly."

"But that's not because I didn't want to fall in love. I was just too busy."

"And why is that?"

Because he'd been determined to prove to Finn Delancy he was worthy of his respect, but he couldn't tell Tony this. "I don't know."

"Yes, you do."

"No, I don't."

"Because you were terrified you'd screw it up."

Liam laughed harshly. "Okay, that's a fact. So what do I do about Katie?"

"Tell her you're falling in love with her."

Liam swallowed. The thought was daunting. "I'm afraid she'll run away."

"Then take her someplace where she can't run away. A place where she has to face her feelings and talk things out with you."

"And where would that be?"

"I dunno. A tropical island."

"You mean, take a vacation?"

"I know that word isn't in your vocabulary, but if you want to romance this woman, then you've got to think of her desires. You both need time away from work and family to create a fantasy world all your own."

It made sense. "But what if she doesn't have real feelings for me?"

"Better to know now and cut things off clean than to keep dating her and hoping she'll start to feel something. It's like a real-estate deal. You're either in or you're out."

Tony was right and Liam knew it, but cutting things off with Katie was easier said than done.

"You gotta take a leap of faith, man," Tony said sagely. "Take a risk with her the way you take a risk on the stock market. Make your plans, do your research, dive in and pray for the best."

"And if I fail?"

"At least you tried. And, hey, I'll be here to help you pick up the pieces."

"Thanks. That means a lot." Liam got to his feet.

Tony came around the desk to punch him lightly on the arm. "Go get her, dude. I'm living proof the rewards are worth the gamble."

_12_

KATIE CAME UP with a brilliant plan for luring Liam to Fiji.

Their mother's will bequeathed the Fiji property equally to Brooke, Joey and Katie. Briefly, they'd discussed the idea of selling it, but so far, none of them had either the heart or the emotional energy to fly out to the Pacific island paradise and check on the bungalow.

She now had the perfect excuse to complete her Martini dare.

There were so many things she wanted to do to Liam. She wanted to sleep with him in a macramé hammock hung between two palm trees. She wanted to make him cry out her name in ecstasy as they made love over the vibrating engine of a snorkel boat. She was dying to do it in a secret alcove of a rocking dance club, in the swimming pool, in the lanai of the bungalow. She fantasized about riding his hard-muscled body in a volcano grotto, beneath a waterfall, in the hot tub.

During her afternoon break, she slipped off to the employee lounge and called him up on her cell phone.

"Liam," she murmured, all hot and bothered by her fantasies.

"Yes." He sounded curt, abrupt. She must have interrupted him in the middle of his work. She almost apologized and hung up. But her determination to complete the Martini dare kept her hanging on.

"It's me," she said, then cringed. What if he didn't know who *me* was?

"Katie." His tone immediately melted into a buttery soft timbre.

Did the sound of her voice make him as horny as the sound of his voice made her? "Did I catch you at a bad time?"

"I was about to go into a meeting, but I have a few minutes. What's up?"

"Um…since you're an expert on real estate, I was hoping you might be willing to give me your opinion on some property my mother left me and my sisters. We're considering selling it, but we don't know if that's the best way to go. Do you think you might be able to look at it for us?"

"Sure," he said. "Where's the property?"

"Um…that's the thing."

"Oh?"

"It's in Fiji."

"As in South Pacific Fiji?"

"Uh-huh. I'd pay for your airplane ticket, of course. We can stay at the bungalow. I can put in for three vacation days and we could make a long weekend of it." *Please, please let him say yes.*

She heard his intake of breath and she could almost see him standing there, thinking about the work he'd be leaving behind if he took off for five days. Was his attraction to her strong enough to overcome his addiction to his work?

"You could have your own room," she ventured. "Keep this strictly a business trip."

"Now, why in the hell would I want to do that?" he asked.

Glee tickled down inside her. She grinned. How she wished he was with her so she could fling her arms around his neck and kiss that firm, angular mouth of his.

"So you'll go?"

"Under one condition."

Her heart squeezed. She held her breath. "What's that?"

"We take my private jet."

THE VIEW OF Fiji Island from the window of Liam's jet was breathtaking. The water was a mesmerizing color of turquoise, the sky cloudless. Even from the air, you could make out the lush growth of brilliantly colored flowers—bougainvillea, anthurium, birds-of-paradise, a stunning palette of red, yellow, orange and green.

Luxury hotels with private bungalows ringed the beach among a proliferation of palm trees. The smell of plumeria blossoms filled the air the minute they stepped onto the tarmac. In the terminal, they were greeted by smiling hostesses with leis made of orchids, along with the soothing, rhythmic sounds of island music. The scenery was so beautiful it felt surreal.

They had taken off from Boston nineteen hours earlier, but the flight had been so much fun it had seemed like nineteen minutes. They'd talked and played cards, watched in-flight movies, napped, eaten filet mignon, drank wine and talked some more.

She found out his favorite actor was Tom Hanks and she confessed to having a mad crush on Orlando Bloom. She learned he liked his steaks well done while she preferred hers rare. He was a whiz at gin rummy, but she thrashed him soundly at poker. But when she suggested a hand of strip poker, Liam refused because he knew he'd end up naked within five hands. Katie told him that was the point.

They'd also done a little kissing—okay, they'd done a *lot* of kissing—but that was all. Even though Katie had tried her best to initiate him as an official member of the mile-high club, Liam had been equally determined to hold her off. His theory was they'd heighten their enjoyment of this trip by making her wait for sex.

They grabbed a cab at the airport and Katie gave the driver directions to her family's bungalow on the beach. It was tucked into a quiet area. Liam carried their bags inside and Katie immediately ran to open the sliding partition that opened out onto a large private lanai. The ocean rolling softly against the shore lulled them with a sweet hypnotic sound.

"I forgot how beautiful it is here." She sighed and breathed in a deep draw of air as she stood looking out at the beach. "We used to come here every summer when my father was alive."

"You miss him, don't you?"

"Something fierce. He was a great father. Strict but fair."

"I wish I knew what that was like," he said. "Having a father's love."

"I wish you did, too."

Liam studied her and his heart reeled. She looked incredible in a pair of white denim shirt shorts and a tangerine halter top with her hair pulled back into a girl-next-door ponytail. No one could have known just by looking at her that she was a Boston blue blood.

This was it, his big chance to take their relationship to a new level. But was she ready? Could he convince her he was a man worth overcoming her fear of commitment for? He prayed he could.

Liam realized how much his outlook on life had changed since he'd met her. Suddenly, something was more important than his work and she was standing right in front of him.

She turned in the doorway to grin over her shoulder at him. Damn if her smile didn't warm him from the inside out.

He grinned back.

She crooked her finger at him. "Come 'ere."

Liam sauntered over.

Katie wrapped her arms around his waist, leaned back to look up into his face. "Let's have sex on the lanai."

"Whoa, slow down. We just got here."

She reached up to stroke her index finger down the length of his cheek. "You're doing this on purpose," she said, pretending to pout.

"Doing what?"

"Withholding sex to tease me."

"Yes, I am," he admitted. "There's something to be said for delayed gratification."

"How long are you planning on holding out on me?"

"For a while."

"You sure you want to get into this?" Her eyes danced.

"Get into what?"

"Making me beg for sex. Because buddy, two can play that game."

"Yeah?"

She licked her lips. "Yeah."

"Go ahead, hit me with your best shot."

"Oh, it's on," she said, and proceeded to untie the string of her halter top.

"What are you doing?"

"What does it look like I'm doing?"

"Getting naked."

"Give the man a cigar." She grinned and let her top drop to the floor.

Liam ogled as she reached for the zipper of her white denim shorts. Did the woman have any idea how hot she was making him?

She wriggled out of her shorts and kicked them across the room. She stood, hands on her hips, wearing nothing but a skimpy peach-colored strapless bra and matching thong panties. In her navel, she sported the cutest little gold ring.

Sassily, she stuck out her tongue, and then reached around to unhook her bra. She twirled it over her head a few times before tossing it in his direction.

"It's not working," Liam said through gritted teeth. He could handle this. Yes, he could.

"Coulda fooled me with that world-class boner." She cast a knowing glance at the zipper of his pants, strained with the outline of his rock-hard erection.

She shimmied out of her panties and strutted out onto the lanai naked as the day she came into the world.

He followed her. The sun was warm on his skin, the ocean spray salty against his tongue. Watching Katie's bottom twitch as she strode toward the lounge chair at poolside, experiencing his desire for her rocketing hard, made Liam feel as if he were a one-celled animal, responding to every stimuli.

Everything about her was intoxicating—the wave of her hips, the perky jut of her breasts, the patch of pecan-blond hair curling at the apex of her thighs.

Glancing over her shoulder again, she gave him a saucy wink and settled herself down on the chaise lounge, legs provocatively spread. She wet her index with her mouth, and then slowly trailed it down to her breasts.

She was driving him insane.

Every whim of her body made the hairs on his wrist quiver. Every vagary of sunlight dappling across her sumptuous breasts registered spiky and vibrant on his retina. Sensation after sensation washed over him. Nothing was lost in translation.

His senses were on high alert, his body tuned for pleasure.

She looked at him with an extraordinary light in her eyes. It worried him and he evaluated her, trying to decode what was going on inside her head. His body took stock of his surroundings, of this moment, like a strong but cautious corporate raider moving through an intri-

cate negotiation, searching for hidden agendas and sub-
terfuge. The novelty of her, the surprise of the expression she was giving him, riveted him.

Life had taught him to be wary. His mother had
taught him to be strong and in control. It was difficult
for him to drop his emotional armor and allow her to see
his vulnerabilities. But he was willing.

Too willing.

She astonished him. Not only by her stunning indi-
viduality but also by the way she made him feel special.
He had to face up to what was happening inside him,
but at the same time he feared it.

It was time to let go of his fears. Time to understand
there was something valuable to be had in this experience.
Time to realize there was always something new to learn,
always valuable insights to be gained. His life did not have
to be buried in work, success and the pursuit of revenge.

"Make love to me, Liam," she begged.

"Dammit, woman." His cock throbbed as he watched
her touch herself.

"You know what you gotta do to have me."

Liam stalked across the patio. He grabbed her by the
shoulders, pinned her against the chaise and kissed her
with a fierceness that pulled a feral growl from his throat.

Katie let out a soft, whispered breath.

In that moment, her small sigh told him something
important. She had goaded him into this because whenever things started to get emotionally intimate between
them, she reached for a physical remedy.

Katie Winfield, he now recognized, was afraid of her
tender feelings.

The seductress image was all a ruse, a protective defense mechanism she hid behind. She cloaked her real self with sexy clothing, adventurous sex and casual relationships. The real Katie disappeared inside parties and flirtatious behavior and frisky role-playing. But there was so much more to her than her sexuality.

Here, with his body pressed against her, he could feel the emotional surging of this deeper, richer, more complex personality. He wondered if she even understood the dynamics of her alluring behavior. Somehow, he doubted it.

Liam felt himself dragged down into the tempting whirlpool of mystery. They stared into each other's eyes and his world narrowed to one simple thing.

Katie.

She was right. He couldn't resist her.

Compelled, Liam scooped a giggling Katie into his arms and carried her back toward the bedroom. She nibbled on his upper arm, driving him straight to distraction. He couldn't wait to get out of his clothes and into her.

He laid her gently down on the bed, but immediately, she popped to her feet.

"Let's do it on the floor." With a wicked gleam in her eyes, she reached for his belt buckle.

"The bed's more comfortable," he said, tussling his T-shirt over his head as she pulled his belt through the loops in a sensuous slither of leather.

"The floor's more adventuresome." She undid the snap on his jeans.

"Adventuresome sex makes me come too fast. For

once, I want to take things nice and slow." He kicked off his shoes. "Which is damned hard to do."

"How about on the bathroom counter in front of the mirror?" She tugged down his zipper.

"How about you resting on fresh sheets with a pillow tucked under your beautiful butt while I find new ways of pleasuring you with my tongue?" He wriggled his eyebrows suggestively.

"How about in the swimming pool?" She tugged both his jeans and his underwear down his hips in one fluid motion, releasing his aching erection from its restraints.

Liam kicked out of the jeans. Feeling giddier than he had the first time he'd made love, he flung himself onto the bed, grinned at her wolfishly and patted the spot beside him. "Come here, Miss Winfield."

KATIE SHOOK her head. Her throat constricted and her fingers went inexplicably numb. "How about we do it on the kitchen table?"

He lay on his side, propped up on his elbow. He looked like a lion, long and lean and powerful. "I know you like adventure, sweetheart, but there's something to be said for tradition. Let's just rock this bed till the slats break."

Sweetheart.

It was the first time Liam had ever called her *sweetheart*. The word formed a precious knot of terror inside her stomach.

She shook her head. "How about in the shower?"

Liam sat up, cocked his head and gave her the strangest look. "What's wrong with the bed?"

Katie shrugged. How could she begin to explain this

nameless sense of dread at the thought of sinking down onto the mattress with him?

A look of sudden insight crossed his face. "You're afraid to make love in a bed."

"I'm not," Katie denied.

"Then prove you're not afraid. Come here."

Katie stayed at the door. Her knees wavered strange and loose and her hands were shaking. "I don't have to prove anything to you."

"Why, you're stone-cold terrified."

"No one is scared of making love in a bed," she scoffed, but her voice came out breathless, airy.

He held out a hand, curled his fingers in a come-hither gesture.

She hung back.

"What's wrong? I thought you were hot for this?"

She shrugged.

"Katie?"

"It just feels weird."

"It's not weird. You're used to hiding behind masks and darkened movie theatres and the shadow of midnight."

"Not necessarily."

"And you like it hard and fast and anonymous. When you have sex, you pretend to be someone else, don't you? A French maid, a 1920s movie siren, a good-girl blue blood gone bad."

"I don't," she squeaked.

"What are you so afraid of, Katie?" he murmured.

"I'm not afraid," she denied. But it was true. All of it. She'd never made love in a bed and she preferred having wild, quick sex in adventurous places while role-playing. "I like sex to be exciting and spontaneous and innovative and—"

"Impersonal," he finished.

"That's not what I was going to say."

"Maybe not, but it's accurate."

Until this moment, until he'd called her on it, she'd never caught on that she avoided having sex in a bed. She thought it was because she was impulsive and creative, but now she knew that wasn't the truth. Now she understood the reason why she'd eschewed beds for floors and swimming pools and closets and movie theatres. Why risk and danger and quick, hurried mating with men she barely knew had been her modus operandi.

Beds were where married people made love. Beds were for committed, long-term relationships. And she just didn't have that kind of staying power. Everyone said so.

"What are you so afraid of?" Liam repeated

You! The way you make me feel. The stark terror that if I let myself love you, somehow I'll lose who I am.

He swung his legs over the bed, got up and stalked toward her, his naked, erect penis bouncing jauntily with every step.

Katie took a step back from him until her bare bottom butted up against the door. She wanted to turn and flee, but Liam wasn't about to let her get away.

He planted both hands against the door over her head, leaned in, lowered his head and looked deeply into her eyes. "I understand you completely, Katie Winfield. Maybe even better than you understand yourself."

Hypnotized, she stared into his eyes, waiting for him to tell her what was wrong with her.

"Doesn't it get tiring?" he asked.

His question was unexpected and made her feel as if he were peeling off the edges of her skin, digging for the woman who lay beneath the surface. Her throat was closing off.

"What?" she whispered.

"Staying in motion, staying busy, trying to outrun your feelings."

"I'm not…" Katie broke off at the tenderness in his eyes. She couldn't talk against the pressure weighing down on her chest.

"It's okay to be ordinary," he murmured. "It's okay for things to be boring once in a while. There's nothing wrong with taking a time out. In fact, when you slow down, you're really able to experience your adventures."

"Oh, that's rich." Her laugh sounded hollow. "Coming from you, Mr. Workaholic."

"Hey, it's the lesson you taught me. You've helped me to realize, all work and no play makes Liam a dull boy. But what I'm trying to tell you is that all go and no staying power makes Katie incomplete. Slow down with me, sweetheart. Let's explore this whole new experience together."

As she looked into his eyes, she knew he saw her for who she really was. He saw past the flirtation and the fun and the flair for the dramatic. He saw the vulnerable Katie who was hiding behind a live-for-today motto. He knew her.

To the very essence of her soul.

Tears rolled slowly down her cheeks. Liam dipped

his head and kissed them away. Then he gently lifted her up into his arms again and took her back to the bed.

This time, she didn't protest.

"Just look into my eyes until the fear passes," he said. "You're safe. I've got you."

Katie smiled up at him through a mist of tears. He settled her against the pillows, tenderly brushing his fingers through her hair.

He was watching her, his eyes taking in every curve and dip of her body. His glance traveled from her shoulders, to her breast, to her waist and lower, up and down the length of her legs. Then stopping to linger a moment at the blond apex between her thighs.

Awareness and a dazzling heat prickled her skin. She'd never felt so exposed. She'd thought that night he'd taken her on top of the Lamborghini was sexually charged. But that time, because he'd taken her from behind, she'd been unable to read his reaction to her body. Now, she saw every erotic thought that crossed his face.

And she understood fully the power she held over him. It simply blew her away.

Her body ignited with the heat of his gaze. That unabashed stare of appreciation caused her heart to knock against her rib cage.

He kissed her lightly, sweetly, drawing it out.

"That's it sweetheart," he said when she moaned softly. "Relax and enjoy every minute of this. We've got all weekend and then some."

Lowering his head, Liam pressed his lips to her bare belly and then kissed his way back up to her nipples, which were aching with desire.

She quivered at the luscious sensation.

"How's that feel?"

"Mmm." It was all she could manage.

He flicked his tongue over one straining bud and then carefully bit down. Reedy blades of pleasure sliced deliriously throughout her breast. She moaned louder.

"You like?"

"No."

"No?" He stopped.

"I love," she purred.

He grinned and went back to work—his mouth suckling, his tongue caressing, fingers tickling.

Brilliant. It felt like shooting stars.

After a long, leisurely exploration that left her hauling in shallow gasps of air, he left her nipples and traveled downward. He spent some time at her navel, playing with that little gold hoop, teasing it in and out of his mouth. The gentle pulling sensation produced crazy, erotic ripples in her belly that undulated all the way down into her throbbing clit.

When his lips reached her straining, hungry clit, he stopped short of touching her with his tongue. His breath was hot against her sensitive flesh, inflaming her beyond understanding.

She arched her hips again, trying to bring his mouth and her clit into contact but he moved with her, keeping his mouth just out of her reach.

"Brute."

He laughed.

"You enjoy torturing me."

"Oh, yeah," Liam admitted. "Stick with me, sweetheart. We'll get there and I promise you it will be worth the wait."

She didn't want to wait. She wanted him to make love to her with his mouth right this very minute. Her brain glazed with lust, her blood pumped feverishly.

Gingerly, Liam spread her thighs wider and moved his body around so that he was positioned between her legs. "So beautiful," he murmured.

The head of his cock throbbed against her knee as he leaned forward. Katie's excitement catapulted. What sweet, desperate pressure.

His big fingers caressed her clit as his tongue probed her folds. Katie's eyes slid closed, blocking out everything except his touch.

"Yes," she whispered. "Yes."

His tongue captured her hooded cleft.

Never in all her life had she been pleasured this way. It was rapture. It was ecstasy.

Liam seemed to know exactly what she needed even better than she knew herself. He reveled in her and he made her feel cherished. It was dangerous territory, these tender feelings, but she couldn't stop them, so she rode, letting the anxiety build, experienced it and then allowed it to drop away.

While he toyed with her clit, Liam slipped an index finger into her slick, wetness. The walls of her womanhood tugged at him, gripping and kneading him in rhythmic waves, pulling his finger deeper and deeper into her.

Sound was altered and she existed in the delicious void of ocean waves and heavy breathing. She floated, bodyless. She was total awareness, her entire being a giant throb of sexual energy.

She surfed his tongue, owned it. She hovered on the brink of orgasm, but he would not let her experience release. A steady strumming vibration began deep in her throat, emerging as a wild moan.

"Liam, Liam," she cried his name.

"What is it, sweetheart?"

"Make me come."

He let loose then, giving her everything, holding nothing back. His tongue danced, his fingers manipulated. She let go and allowed him to take over. It seemed he was everywhere. Over her, around her, in her, outside of her.

He was magic. He was wonder. He was amazing.

"More." She thrashed her head. "More, more. Give me more."

He gave it to her just the way she asked for it, pumping his hand into her with his fingers. His thumb pressed her clit like a trigger, shooting off the secret button of her release.

"Come Katie, come for me," he coaxed.

She exploded.

The orgasm overtook her in great, writhing pleasure moans.

She cried out, her voice echoing around the room. Laying there, she trembled with the power of what he'd just done to her.

And she realized that making love in a bed hadn't been boring or predictable or uninspired. In fact, it had been the most intimate, intense, moving experience of her life.

13

LIAM TOOK HER to dinner at an elegant restaurant, specializing in Pacific fusion, not far from the bungalow. Utilizing indigenous seafood, the chef paired French cooking and Asian flavors. Adventuresome Katie ordered squid and sushi. Liam, sticking with more traditional fare, went with the tuna.

They were seated at the best table near a romantic waterfall surrounded by exotic vegetation. He looked dashing in his suit, although she couldn't wait until she could get him out of it again.

Liam ate like a man whose appetite had been whetted. Tilting her head, she watched him in the candlelight and couldn't believe she'd underestimated his passion. This was a man who could really enjoy himself when he allowed his playful side to come out.

Briefly, they discussed both his ad campaign—which was almost finished—and the bungalow's profitability. Liam's opinion was that her family could make more by keeping the bungalow and renting it out than by selling it. Then, he presented the downside to renting versus selling. But this dinner wasn't about business and they both knew it.

"Which way would *you* go do you think?" Katie quizzed. "Sell or rent?"

"When you've got something valuable, you should hang on to it." He was gazing at her, and she knew he wasn't talking about real estate.

"Is that the outlook that turned you into a tycoon?"

"No. What's got me where I am today is recognizing a great opportunity when it falls into my lap."

Katie felt a blush of heat radiate up her neck. The more she was around him, the more she found to like and admire. He was strong and masculine, but also tender and kind. And he made her hope for something she'd never hoped for in her life.

She savored her dessert of bananas foster while Liam sipped a brandy. He raised his glass and winked at her.

Katie winked back, noticing how his hazel eyes darkened with appreciation whenever he looked at her.

He paid for the meal against her protest that she owed him for flying all the way to Fiji to assess her family's property, but he hushed her by saying, "We both know that's not why you invited me. Nor was it the reason I came."

For one heart-stopping moment, she thought he knew about her Martini dare, but she quickly realized that was impossible. She'd almost forgotten about the silly dare herself.

He held out his hand to her as they left the restaurant. "Stroll on the beach?"

"How about skinny-dipping in the moonlight?"

"To be honest," he said, "I never found sex on a beach quite what it's cracked up to be. Too much sand in all the wrong places, and now that I've been introduced to the wonders of regular bed sex, I don't want us to lose our momentum."

"Okay," she agreed without protest because she was enjoying the bed sex more than she wanted to let on. She slipped her arm through his, snuggled up close against his warm body. Sated happiness, sweet and light, filtered from her head to her toes.

When they reached the sand, Katie took off her sandals and hooked them around two fingers. Hand in hand they walked along the beach, the surf lapping at their feet.

The night breeze was balmy, but the heat rolling off his body was sizzling. Her own body heat was inching upward as she thought about what would happen when they got back to the bungalow. Every time she caught a whiff of his cologne, she felt a jolt of desire deep inside.

She loved the feelings he generated, wished she could feel them forever. He let go of her hand to slip his arm around her waist, and she rested her head on his shoulder.

Fifteen minutes later, having gotten their fill of ocean and moonlight, they picked their way up the path to the bungalow.

Liam took the keys from her, unlocked the door and held it open for her. Once they'd crossed the threshold, he drew her into the circle of his embrace. While he kissed her, he inched down the zipper on the back of her aqua-and-white floral sheath dress.

Every nerve in her body came alive. Katie shivered as his mouth moved slowly from her lips to her chin to the smooth column of her throat. Her dress slipped off her shoulders, fell past her hips. Dreamily, she stepped out of it.

Wearing only panties and pearls, she turned to unbutton Liam's crisp white shirt. Once the buttons were undone, and she wrested the shirt off his shoulders, Katie splayed her hands and pushed her palms over his bare chest.

"Ssss," she hissed in appreciation. "I love your chest."

"No more than I love yours," he said, and cupped her breasts in his hands.

She giggled and reached for the waistband of his pants.

Liam took her hand and led her slowly into the bedroom. This time, she did not try to avoid the bed.

"You know," she whispered as he laid her down, "you're the only man I've ever made love to in a bed."

"I kind of figured."

"How did you know?"

He kissed her forehead. "You can't hide anything from me, Katie Winfield."

Suddenly, she didn't *want* to hide anything from him. She wanted to tell him everything. All her secrets, all her shame. But their bodies were too fired up for more conversation.

They were looking at each other and their tandem breathing quickened. Falling and rising in spiky inhalations and shuddered releases. The moonlight streaming in through the lanai sensitized their sense of touch, taste, hearing and smell.

His palms weren't calloused, but they were manly—strong and flat—as they skimmed over her breasts. The sound he made had her picturing a panther prowling his cage. And his scent—so masculine and musky it filled her nose and stirred her libido.

He pulled her up tight against his chest, pressing her to his hard angles that promised so much enjoyment. She tilted her head and planted a kiss on his chin.

Their chemistry took over and they descended into rapture.

Katie whimpered in desperation. She wanted to feel him the way he was feeling her. She gripped his hard-muscled back, dug her fingernails into his skin. Desire rolled through her veins, tugged her down on an upsurge of sexual need. Tossed her heedlessly toward a destiny she couldn't fathom but lusted after. Her sex clenched hard, eager to meld with his.

His erection stabbed through his briefs, the hard ridge of him pushing against exactly the right spot on her.

Katie moaned soft and low. She swayed into him, bumping her hips against his.

He nibbled her earlobe, growled into her ear. A lightning bolt of desire shot straight to her womb. He brought his pelvis hard into hers, his erection poking provocatively, offering erotic possibilities of what was to come.

Katie wanted to feel him inside her. She was overtaken by the feeling, flooded with need and being needed. There was no restraint.

She wanted it.

Wanted him.

Wanted to feel everything all at once.

She grabbed the top of his briefs and pulled them down. He helped her, kicking them over his feet.

Naked together again.

He touched her, gently pushing his thick middle finger inside of her, stroking her ache.

She nipped his shoulder and then sank her teeth lightly into his flesh.

He touched her in places that ignited thoughts of what it would feel like when he was between her thighs, pushing deep enough inside her to soothe that throbbing ache.

She stroked his erection. He pulsed and throbbed against her hand. His entire body shuddered.

"Condom?" she whispered.

"I've got it."

His mouth caught hers again in a possessive kiss that made her quiver. Caught her, arrested her. They were swept up by a maelstrom of passion. Completely and utterly vulnerable to each other.

Her fingers tingled to skate down those masculine curves and hard-muscled ridges.

He clamped a hand around her bottom and drew her up tight against his hardness and she melted. Into him, into the darkness of midnight.

Liam leveled himself into her, slipping in with surprisingly gentle movements considering how fired up they both were.

She hissed in a breath. The minute Liam was snug inside, her muscles contracted around him.

"Oh, no, ma'am, don't start that yet," he said, "or I won't last a minute."

But he felt so good, so big and thick that she couldn't resist squeezing.

Slowly, he began to move. Their bodies fit. Hand in glove.

"What a woman," he growled. "You are magnificent."

He cupped her chin with his palm, raised her face up, rained kisses onto her chin. Her eyelids, her nose, her cheeks, her forehead. Then he took her mouth again, kissing her more deeply than she ever thought possible. Taking her breath, taking her heart, taking everything she had.

She felt every manly inch of him as he slid in and out of her warm moist folds, his movements languid and pointed. Clearly designed to drive her quite mad. She could feel it coming, gathering in her womb, rumbling up from deep within her.

His thrusts lengthened, and she wrapped her arms around his neck, holding on for dear life.

Legs braced wide, penis sliding in and out of her, Liam anchored her to the mattress, his strong arms holding her in place. Like a dedicated explorer, he took his time, gradually getting to know the feel of her.

She slid the fingers of one hand down his back, feeling the bumps in his spine, grateful for him, for this moment, for this delicious pleasure.

They kissed repeatedly, their mouths coming together for a quick taste of heaven, and then pulling apart on a sigh as activities demanded.

They glided together under the covers, writhing, mating, swept up in the heat, the intensity, the slick seduction.

His thrusts quickened. She egged him on with hot little gasps and soft, hungry moans. Her contractions gripped him tight, pulling him deep within her. Holding on for dear life, she whispered his name over and over again.

Tension mounted.

Liam drove into her. Forceful now, demanding. His early gentleness evaporating in the face of urgent need.

She tightened her legs around his waist. He fondled her buttocks in his hand, spearing her hard, banging into her.

The inside of her thighs rode his hips. Relentlessly.

She could feel his legs quivering, knew he was on the verge of climax. It was gonna be big.

They exploded, shattering into pieces, the orgasm tearing through them simultaneously. She felt it ripple from her womb. Felt the shot of his heat flood through her.

At that very moment, Katie fell deeply in love.

LIAM HAD NEVER FELT happier in his life. He propped himself up on one elbow and lay watching her sleep, his eyes tracing the outlines of her dear face.

She'd spoiled him for good. After her, no other woman could ever compare.

And he was deliriously happy about his ruination.

To his mind, Katie was the sexiest woman in the world and he wanted her all the time. They had such fun together. Both in bed and out of it. He admired the way life delighted her. And her unfettered heart unfettered him.

Her impulses were elegant, lovely things, and it was troublesome, but astonishing, to appreciate the way she managed him. It wasn't deviousness on her part. It was just the way she was and she had him twisted around her little finger.

Because of his past and his issues with Finn Delancy,

Liam feared he might never be able to able to have an open and honest relationship with a woman. But his growing feelings for Katie overrode his trepidation. His need for connection was stronger than his fears that he didn't measure up.

Liam acknowledged that she needed more time, that her own fear of commitment wouldn't disappear over night. That was fine. He had all the patience in the world. In the meantime, he was determined to show her exactly how much she meant to him.

And that she could depend on him to be there for her, no matter what.

LATER, Katie woke to find Liam's leg thrown over her waist, his hair sexily ruffled, his gaze fixed upon her face. She closed her eyes and smiled when he leaned over to kiss her.

She had to admit it. They were glorious together. Sex with Liam was the best she'd ever had.

He nuzzled her cheek lightly. She lifted her lashes partway, still smiling, and slanted him a flirtatious glance.

The way he looked at her made her feel as if she were the sexiest woman who'd ever lived. She thought she knew her body well, but through the lens of his eyes, she was different. Unknown to herself. And he was adventurously charting her unexplored territories.

Liam pulled her close. She rested her nose against his collarbone, smelling his essence, resting her chin against his curly black chest hairs. They lay unmoving, enrapt by the sounds of their own heartbeats.

Slowly, she became fully aware of the weight of their

touching bodies. She eased from the circle of his arms, kissing his skin as she went.

Eyes flashing, he edged his fingertips up the slope of her inner thigh, tickling her.

Katie's laugh, thick and erotic, oozed out into the room. She sounded husky and languid, as if she were changing, becoming someone new.

And Liam was the channel, guiding her into being more than she'd ever thought she could be.

In the process, she was learning to let go of her need for constant excitement, adventure and stimulation. Learning she could, indeed, trust these tender feelings swelling inside her. Liam had brought her to his bed, brought her into the daylight. He'd taken away her deepest fear—that she had no staying power for the long haul.

She grasped his shoulders to steady the fluttering of her pulse against the tingling of his gentle strokes. He rested his head against her belly. Her breath came quicker, deeper. A thrust of understanding expanded her heart.

He raised his head to look at her. They gazed deeply into each other's eyes. Not saying a word, just taking each other in. Katie spied something that she'd never seen in a man's eyes after lovemaking. It was a certainty. A knowing that only true and honest loyalty could bring.

What did her eyes say to him? Could he tell that he'd changed her? Could he see that she was letting down her guard, letting him in, going where she'd never gone with any man before?

Respect passed between them. A promise yet unspoken, but solidly real.

His erection stirred against her thigh, growing hard

and hot all over again. She reached down to caress him, admiring his size and texture.

Anticipation sparked in his eyes as she increased the measured stroking, cupping his balls in her other hand. She delighted at the way they drew up against his crotch. Instantly, she felt a corresponding pressure, a tightening of her own nerve endings.

She bent her head. Kissed his satiny tip, tasted his pungent tang. She slid her tongue down one side of him, tracing his pattern.

He groaned.

Her tongue traveled, roaming over the brilliant territory. As her excitement grew, her control slipped. Her mouth closed delicately over the head of him.

Liam lay motionless, straining against his impulses. She clutched his hips with both hands, sucked him first slowly all the way to his tip, turning her head so she could feel every part of him, then slipping down to the base of his shaft.

Katie dove, her tongue swirling, in one fluid movement.

Sitting up, she moved her hands around his buttocks to the inside of his firm, muscular thighs. Gently, she stroked, moving over him with a shivering lightness. She glided with him.

Yet the whole time she was holding back, holding something in reserve. Their pace quickened and they never lost contact. They swayed in unison.

"Katie, Katie, Katie," he groaned, his head thrown back, his eyes tightly closed.

His body went rigid. The signal she was looking for. The signal to wait.

Katie did not move, her mouth resting on the base of his shaft, the head of him throbbing inside her.

He shuddered in premonition.

She wrapped her legs around his thighs so he could feel her warm wetness, dripping with excitement. She undulated her hips in rhythm with her mouth, moving up and down him once more.

His hands reached for her. He touched her hair. His fingers moved blindly over her shoulders, trying to find a place to hold on to as he arched his back.

She wriggled away from his hands, determined to focus all her attention on his pleasure, knowing he would return it tenfold. She closed her eyes, calmed her pulsating heart. All her consciousness pooled in her fingers and her tongue.

He was close. So very close.

His breath came in rough gasps. Her body simmered in sweet sweat as they rocked together. She moved her mouth and her fingers took over. With a burst and shudder, he came, his juices leaking over her hand onto his belly.

He cried her name.

And she collapsed against him. Together, they lay breathing heavily, absorbed by ecstasy, until slowly they slipped into a deep, dreamless sleep.

WHEN KATIE WOKE again, dawn was rising on the sky-light beyond the lanai. The morning breeze was slight. Birds chirped happily in the palm trees, greeting the new day.

Beside her, Liam slept like a sexually satisfied male—lying on his stomach, arm slung over a pillow, his gorgeously naked butt on delicious display. Grinning, she slipped out of bed, careful not to awaken him and padded naked into the kitchen to put on the coffee.

After a night of rigorous sex, Katie was feeling a tad achy. She pulled a bottle of water from the fridge and twisted off the top. She found her purse—after stepping over the pile of clothes they'd left scattered at the front door—and dug for a travel bottle of ibuprofen.

As she did, her fingers brushed the corners of the pink envelope from Lindsay Beckham.

Her third Martini dare.

The first two had turned out so splendidly, she was intrigued to discover what the third dare entailed. She swallowed two of the pills and put on Liam's discarded white shirt. The hem of it hit at the middle of her thigh, and it smelled of him. She pressed the collar to her nose and inhaled the scent of him as she sat down on the sofa. She propped her bare feet on the coffee table and slid her fingernail under the flap of the envelope.

Out fell the parchment scroll wrapped with the familiar red velvet ribbon.

She untied the ribbon and unrolled the scroll to read one single word.

Confess.

Confess? Confess what? To whom?

Puzzled, Katie peered into the envelope in hopes there was something else inside, but it was empty.

"Morning, early bird, I smell coffee brewing."

She looked up to see Liam standing in the entry way, his hair disheveled, sheet creases on his cheek, looking totally adorable. Her heart melted all over again.

"Hey." He grinned. "You look much better in my shirt than I ever did."

She smiled at his compliment.

He yawned and scratched his chest. A total guy. "Watcha got there?"

All at once it was perfectly clear what she was supposed to confess and to whom. "It's a Martini dare."

"What's a Martini dare?" he asked, picking his underwear and pants up off the floor and sliding into them.

"It's something I have to do for this women's club I joined. They dare you to do something outside your comfort zone." She went on to explain the tenets of Martinis and Bikinis.

He sat down beside her on the couch and reached for his shoes. "Sounds interesting."

"It is."

He leaned over her shoulder, peered at the scroll. "Confess? What does that mean?"

Katie swallowed. She had a sudden fear Liam wasn't going to take this dare in the spirit she'd agreed to do it. "I think I'm supposed to confess to you."

He went suddenly still, one shoe off and one shoe on. "Confess what?"

"That you're my Martini dare."

He drilled a hole through her with his eyes. "What do you mean?"

"Remember that afternoon in the theatre?"

"How could I possibly forget?"

"It was a Martini dare."

"They dared you to have sex with me?"

"In a forbidden place."

He looked as if someone had just kicked him in the gut. "And this trip to Fiji?"

Feeling miserable, she nodded. "Have sex in an exotic place."

He clamped his lips together and said not another word. He got up off the couch and went to the bedroom. Katie jumped up to follow him. "It was stupid, I know."

He didn't even look at her, just stalked to bathroom, and scooped his toothbrush and razor off the counter.

"What...what are you doing?"

"What does it look like?" he snapped, picking his suitcase up off the floor and stuffing his toiletries inside.

"You're leaving?"

"Yes." His jaw tightened as he bent over to zip up his suitcase.

She stared at him. "But why?"

"You lured me here on false pretenses."

"Oh, come on, you didn't come here just to assess the value of my family's real estate."

He straightened up to glare at her. "No, I came here because you and my best friend convinced me I needed to learn how to relax. That I needed to take a vacation. I came here because..." He shook his head. "Forget it."

This wasn't making sense. She couldn't understand why he was so furious with her. Okay, so her dares were a little underhanded, but they weren't malicious. They'd both had a good time. Why weren't they laughing about this over the breakfast buffet?

She touched his forearm, but he shook her off. "What is it?"

His glower cut her like a knife. "I came here because I thought you and I might have a future together. I knew it was going to be tough. I knew you were commitment-phobic, I knew I was taking a chance by laying my heart on the line, but I had no idea you were toying with me. That I was nothing more to you than some stupid dare."

"You are more to me than a stupid dare."

"Then why didn't you just tell me about it?"

"We're supposed to keep the dares a secret," she said. "Club rules."

"And you put your oath to your Martini club above my feelings?"

"I admit it. You're right. I should have told you about the dare before I invited you out here. I made mistake."

"Damn right you did."

Stupefied, Katie couldn't speak. She stared at him, openmouthed.

His eyes flared with anger. "You don't get it, do you?"

"No, I don't."

He pressed his lips together in a hard line. "And that's the problem. You don't get me. I can't believe that I ever thought you did."

"Liam, I never meant to hurt you. You've got to believe that."

"I won't be played for a fool, Katie, and I won't tolerate deception in any form. Especially, not from the woman I'm dating." He snatched his suitcase off the bed and carried it out the door.

She stood there dumbfounded, hands on her hips, watching him stride away. She could understand that he didn't think the dare was funny. She could understand why he might be put out, but this angry reaction was over the top.

See, see, this is why you should avoid commitment, shouted the voice that had always kept her from investing in a long-term relationship.

But then another part of her, a wiser part of her she'd never heard before whispered, *This isn't about you. He's got an old wound and you just knocked off the scab.*

When she returned to the living room, she found him on the phone, calling for a taxi to the airport. "You're really doing this. You're really going?"

"Don't worry, I won't leave you stranded," he said as he hung up, forever a man of honor. "I'll take the next commercial flight off the island. I'll leave my jet for you."

"Liam, you're blowing this all out of proportion. You're a rational man, I don't get why you're acting so betrayed." She reached out to grab his wrist and pushed up the wristband of his watch in the process, revealing the tattoo that marked him.

All at once the anger rolled out of him. She could see it in the sag of his shoulders, the tired shake of his head. "I'm sorry, Katie, I thought we had something, but now I see we don't. You're a blue-blooded Brahmin from Beacon Hill and no matter how much money I make I'll always be the gangster kid from the South Boston projects."

"Where you come from doesn't mean a damn thing to me," she cried.

"Maybe not," he said. "But it matters to me."

"Are you breaking up with me?"

He snorted. "How can I be? We were never together. I was only your dare, remember?"

The taxi horn honked outside. He picked up his suitcase, lumbered out of the bungalow.

"Liam, don't leave. We can talk this out. Work it out. Liam, please!"

But he didn't hear her. He was already climbing into the taxi, the sound of the ocean wind blowing her voice back into her face with the cold, hard slap of reality.

The man had just broken her heart.

14

ABOUT HALFWAY over the Pacific, Liam's anger evaporated. He thought of Katie and how forlorn she'd looked standing in the doorway of the bungalow, barefooted and wearing nothing but his white dress shirt.

You did the right thing, he tried to convince himself. How could they have a relationship if she was going to keep secrets from him?

Dude, he could almost hear Tony's voice in his head, *it was just a silly dare. Get over it.*

Liam shook his head. It wasn't the dare that bothered him. It was the level of deception she'd gone to in order to lure him to Fiji. It was the fact that she'd used him for her own gratification while he'd been falling in love with her. He thought of how Arianna had humiliated him back in college. Katie was exactly like her, another privileged female toying with the heart of the boy from the wrong side of the tracks for her own amusement.

That's where you're dead wrong. Katie is nothing like Arianna and you know it.

In fact, Katie was unlike any woman he'd ever met.

She was sweet and lively, imaginative and generous. She threw herself headlong into everything she attempted. She was unusual, intense, complex and gorgeous as all get out. There were so many things he liked about Katie. Her upbeat attitude and how he instantly felt better whenever he was near her. He loved how she surprised and delighted him with her sense of wonder and adventure. He admired her fearlessness in going after what she wanted.

After he'd met her, he'd put his issues with Finn Delancy on hold. For the first time since he'd found out Delancy was his father, his grudge had taken a backseat to something else. Being with Katie had him letting go of his secret shame and embracing life. And for these past few weeks, he'd felt free.

And he'd walked out on her. All because of an idiotic dare.

What in the hell was the matter with him?

"Would you care for something to drink, sir?" asked the flight attendant as she came around the first-class cabin.

"Whiskey," he ordered, hoping the alcohol would take his mind off his mistakes.

He remembered the last time he'd drank whiskey. It had been at Finn Delancy's dinner party. He recalled what had happened later in the park, after he'd confessed his secret to Katie. She'd never judged, just offered her body up to him as solace.

His heart ached and his body tightened with need. Yet he'd never make love to Katie again. Random images of her flashed in his mind—strutting her stuff in that provocative French-maid costume, kicking his butt in bowling, holding his hand as they walked along the beach.

Each freeze-frame tugged at his desire, mocked

his stupidity. It was as if his whole life were looped on instant replay, a poignant déjà vu of how he'd flubbed up.

To distract himself from the pain, he tugged the in-flight magazine from the pocket on the back of the seat in front of him and listlessly leafed through the pages, but it didn't hold his attention.

Liam noticed a man get up and walk down the aisle to the lavatory. A few minutes later, a sexy, long-legged blonde woman followed, squeezing into the same lavatory the man had entered ahead of her.

Clearly, they were angling to become members of the mile-high club. He grinned. It looked like they were in for a fun ride to the States.

Great. He sounded just like Katie. Everything's a lark, even when it's inappropriate or probably illegal.

That's right. Hold on to the negative aspects of her personality. That way you don't have to remember what her lips feel like on yours, or the adorable sounds she makes during sex, or how good it felt to hold her in your arms.

Determined to lose himself in the printed word, Liam purposely forced his attention onto the in-flight magazine. He turned the page.

The headline of the article grabbed hold of his stomach with a vicious twist. TEN BEST U.S. CITY MAYORS. Quickly, his gaze ran down the list. Boston, he perused. Mayor Finn Delancy.

Bitter disgust rose up his throat. Gritting his teeth, he read the article. It was a glowing review of what Delancy had done for the city. But what really chafed Liam was the section on what a fine father Delancy was. There was a picture showing Finn tossing around a football with his teenage sons on the lawn of his Beacon Hill home.

Liam's half brothers.

Emotions he'd been suppressing for three decades fell in on him. He felt cheated, wronged, jealous and unloved. But most of all he felt betrayed. He crumpled the magazine in his fist and closed his eyes. Luckily the seat next to him was empty so he didn't have to defend himself against a prying seatmate.

He reached down deep inside himself, fighting for self-control, trying to tamp down the emotions that until now, he managed to hide under the umbrella of vengeance. He'd wanted to get even with Delancy for betraying him and for hurting his mother.

And then the realization struck him.

He knew why he'd overreacted to Katie's confession that she'd seduced him on a dare. Why he'd felt so deceived. Why he'd always had a difficult time tolerating deception of any kind.

It was because *he'd* been hiding from the truth. He'd been deceiving himself. He'd projected his fears and shortcomings onto Katie.

All these years he'd kept his identity a secret, telling no one who his father was until the night he'd confessed to Katie. Even to himself, he'd denied he was part blue blood, had eschewed that gene of his DNA.

There's only one way around this. Only one way he would find his way back to Katie.

He was going to have to face the man he had become, and to do that he had to confront Delancy.

THE RIBBON-CUTTING ceremony for the Habitat for Humanity project was about to commence as Liam walked up to the site of the new-home construction. A grandstand had been built in front of the buildings, and the media gathered, setting up to film Delancy getting an award.

The irony didn't escape Liam. Thirty-one years ago, his mother had been pregnant, jobless and homeless because Delancy had discarded her like an old shoe after he'd had his way with her. Now here was Delancy, lauded as a champion of the poor and downtrodden because he'd hammered a few nails in a wall.

"Liam." Flanked by his bodyguards, Delancy stepped forward, hand outstretched to greet him. "Glad you could make it."

Liam hesitated before taking Delancy's hand. He didn't want to touch the man, but he knew that he must. In order to move on, in order to heal his troubled soul, he had to forgive this man.

Soldiering past the resentment in his heart, Liam reached out and took Delancy's hand. "Mayor."

"Please, call me Finn. Anyone who donates a hundred thousand dollars to this project deserves to call me by my first name."

"What about your son?" Liam asked. "What does he deserve to call you?"

"Excuse me?" Delancy looked confused.

"My mother is Jeanine James."

Delancy's blank face told Liam he didn't even re-member his mother.

Liam tensed against the rage running through him. He would not lose control. He would not give this man the satisfaction of knowing how much he af-fected him. "Thirty-one years ago you knew her very well."

"Thirty-one years is a long time." Delancy made a noise that sounded like a half laugh, half snort of de-rision. "I've met a lot of people since then."

"You never told her you were married. You wined her, dined her. She was a poor, seventeen-year-old Irish immigrant, and she felt as if she'd won the lottery when you took an interest in her."

"This is a fabrication." Delancy bristled.

"You got her pregnant, then told her to have an abortion."

"I never got any woman pregnant other than my wife, Sutton," Delancy denied.

"When she refused," Liam went on, making sure to keep his tone low and measured, "you ignored her. She had no money, no place to live and she was pregnant with your bastard son."

Delancy's throat worked silently and his face beat bright red. "Nonsense. Utter nonsense."

"I'm your son and I've spent my entire life hating you. I hated you so much I was determined to make something of myself. Determined to convince myself I was better than you. I put myself through Harvard and became a successful businessman. I'm worth almost a billion dollars and I did it because of you."

"Your mother is mistaken. I'm not your father, James," Delancy said coldly.

"Your name is right here on my birth certificate." Liam pulled the birth certificate from his pocket, slapped it in Delancy's hand.

Delancy's bodyguards shifted, moving in closer, getting ready to hustle him off. He shoved the certificate back at Liam. "I don't care what name your mother put on that birth certificate. I'm not your father."

"Prove it." Liam lifted his chin, stared Delancy down. Liam's palms were sweating and his heart was thumping but he'd never felt more like his true self. "Take a DNA test."

"I don't have to prove anything." Delancy turned away from him, turned toward the crowd collecting around the grandstand.

Liam's old need for revenge reared its ugly head.

The temptation was there—a microphone, an audience, the media. All he had to do was walk over to the mike and make the announcement that could shatter Delancy's career. He could spill Finn Delancy's secret all over Boston and finally have his revenge.

But he didn't reach for the microphone. Didn't make the public announcement he'd spent years fantasizing about. He couldn't bring himself to hurt the innocent people involved—Sutton Delancy, his half brothers. But most of all, he couldn't put the scrutiny of the spotlight on his mother. She'd suffered enough because of this thoughtless, vain, self-centered man.

He'd done what he'd come here to do. Delancy knew who he was. That's all that mattered.

As Liam turned and walked down the steps of the grandstand, an immediate lightness filled him. A smile tilted his lips and his heart was flooded with the knowledge that he'd just let himself out of a prison of his own making. Delancy no longer had any hold over him. He was free.

Free to love Katie, wholly, completely without any reservation.

Until now, his identity had been caught up in doing and achieving, trying to prove himself worthy of a man who did not deserve his love. But by facing his demons and confronting Delancy, he was finally able to see the truth of it.

Blue blood or commoner. Rich or poor. Bastard son, recognized or not. He was ten times the man Delancy would ever be.

And he owed it all to Katie for helping him to see who he really was deep down inside. Knowing her, being with her, had changed him forever. Changed him in profound and positive ways.

She'd shown him how to embrace his inner child, to have fun and live in the moment. Strange that he'd accused her of deception because until Katie, there had been no hope of true honesty and genuineness in his life.

Before Katie, he'd been quick and competent and capable. He still was, of course, but making a buck was no longer so important. He no longer had anything to prove. What was important now was being true to what had real value to him.

Katie.

He craved her with a longing beyond reason. He

had to have her and he was going to do everything in his power to win her back.

THE MORNING AFTER she returned from Fiji, Katie trudged into Sharper Designs. The final art design for Liam's campaign was due. It had taken every ounce of courage she possessed to show up at the office today. All she'd wanted to do was call in to work, hide under the covers and huddle there for the rest of her life.

She had the misfortune of falling in love with Liam James. She loved so many things about him—his sense of honor, his work ethic, the way he could see past the boisterous front she put up to hide her fears.

But his emotional stumbling blocks kept tripping them up. He was a loyal and complicated man. His feelings ran deep, but he had buried them under his stiff upper lip so that she didn't believe he was capable of expressing those feelings. And dammit, Katie deserved a man who could tell her what was in his heart.

A few minutes after Katie had slumped in her chair with a mocha latte, Tanisha came bounding through the door, her face all aglow.

"Good morning!" She greeted Katie with a gigantic smile.

"Well—" Katie blinked, feeling a tad bit disappointed by Tanisha's enthusiasm. She had visions of them washing away their man woes together over shots of peppermint schnapps during happy hour at the closest bar. "You look as if you've rebounded nicely from your breakup with Dwayne. Did you have an exciting hookup this weekend?"

"I did." Tanisha grinned slyly, her hands clasped behind her back. "*With* Dwayne."

"You guys made up? That's so wonderful," she said struggling to control her heartache.

"We didn't just make up." Tanisha's eyes danced.

"No?"

"We're getting married!" Tanisha let out a squeal and thrust her left hand under Katie's nose so she could see the big two-carat marquis diamond engagement ring on her finger.

"That's wonderful!" Katie jumped up to give her friend a hug. Truly, she was happy for Tanisha, but there was a pity party going on inside Katie's stomach. She felt so left out.

"He took me to a Red Sox game and there it was up on the scoreboard during the seventh-inning stretch for the whole world to see. *Tanisha, will you marry me?*"

"Ah," Katie said, "the grand gesture."

"Girlfriend, let me tell you, it was a dream come true."

"I thought you told me once that you weren't the marrying kind."

Tanisha waved it off. "That was before I met Dwayne. The right man can change your mind about anything."

"Tell me," Katie muttered. She thought she'd found the right man and she'd changed, but then he'd turned out to be the wrong man and she felt like a total fool for following her heart.

"We're getting married next June," Tanisha chattered. "And, of course, I want you to be my maid of honor."

"Sure, sure." The smile froze to her face.

"I tell you, Katie—" Tanisha grasped both her hands in hers "—I've never been so happy."

"That's wonderful."

Tanisha canted her head. "Are you all right?"

"Fine." Katie forced herself to look perky.

"How was your weekend in Fiji with Liam?"

Katie shook her head. "Don't ask."

"Not good?"

"I don't want to talk about it. This is your day. Tell me all about Dwayne."

Tanisha shook a finger at her. "Nuh-uh. You're not getting off that easy. Something is bothering you. You're not your usual self. Sure, I'm happy, but I want you to know I'm here for you, no matter what. So spill it. What happened in Fiji?"

Katie shrugged, trying to act nonchalant in the hopes that it wouldn't hurt so much. Quickly, she told her about the Martini dares and how she'd used Liam to complete them. And how upset he'd been when she confessed what she'd been up to. "Was I so wrong?" she finished, lacing her fingers together nervously.

"Not to my way of thinking, but some guys have issues about being completely honest."

"Liam is definitely in that camp," Katie said gloomily.

Tanisha shook her head. "I've never seen you this torn up over a man."

"I've never felt like this over a man before."

"Seriously, Katie, you're not going to let this misunderstanding come between you two."

If anyone but Tanisha had told her this, Katie would

have been inclined to make light of her feelings for Liam. But this was Tanisha, who'd started at Sharper Designs on the same day she had. Who'd let her sleep on her couch when Katie's condo was being fumigated. Who brought over Chinese food when she was down in the dumps and doled out sharp-witted advice.

She owed Tanisha the truth. Had to open herself up to someone. Tanisha had proven she was her friend.

"It's too late. I mean, even if he did forgive me for deceiving him, I don't know if *I* can forgive him for walking out on me. The least he could have done was stay and fight."

"Don't judge him too quickly. Some people withdraw when they're upset. That's what happened with Dwayne and me."

"The one time I finally break down and have sex in a bed, I go and fall in love," her voice cracked.

"What?" Tanisha's eyes rounded. "Did you say the L word?"

Miserably, Katie nodded.

"Oh, sweetie," Tanisha said with such a look of pity on her face that Katie wanted to crawl into a hole and pull dirt over her.

All the years she'd spent playing the field and having fun, keeping her heart safely out of the fray, had come to a crashing end. She was no longer immune to the slings and arrows of love.

And it hurt so bad.

"I'm okay. I'll be all right. I don't want to rain on your parade. How about we go out tonight and celebrate your pending marriage."

"Ooh, I'm sorry." Tanisha made a face. "We're going over to my folks to tell them in person. Tomorrow night, maybe?"

"Sure." Katie bobbed her head. Thankfully, her cell phone rang at that moment. She pulled it from her pocket as Tanisha went off to flash her engagement ring to the rest of their coworkers. "Hello?"

"Katie?"

"Yes?"

"This is Lindsay Beckham," came the cool polished voice of the Martinis and Bikinis president.

Great. It was the person responsible for her downfall. "What is it?" she asked, only barely managing to control her snippy tone.

"I'm afraid there's been something of a mix-up."

"A mix-up?"

Lindsay paused. "It's totally my fault. I take full responsibility."

"For what?"

"The last dare I sent you?"

"Yeah?"

"It was meant for one of the other women."

Katie let out a bark of laughter. "That's hilarious."

"Excuse me?"

"Because of that last dare, my life is ruined."

"Ruined?" Lindsay repeated. "Are you sure you're not overstating the issue?"

"You told me to confess!"

"No, I told Sherry to confess."

"But you sent Sherry's dare to me, so it had the same consequences as if you'd sent it to me." Katie's hand was shaking. From anger, from sorrow, from the whole sheer craziness of it. "You know what? I wish I'd never set foot in your bar. I wish I'd never met you and your Martini group."

"This is worse than I thought," Lindsay said. "I'm sorry, I never meant for this to happen. If you'd let me make amends—"

"Nice of you to offer, but unless you know how to superglue a broken heart, there's not much you can do. I've got to get back to work now."

"I hope you won't give up on Martinis and Bikinis just because of this little snafu—"

"Bye," Katie said, and hung up, never feeling more wretched.

IN A VAIN ATTEMPT to boost her spirits, Katie made a beeline for the pet shop after her awful day at work. She couldn't wait for the salve of seeing Duke's sweet face and happily wagging tail.

"Hey, pup," Katie cooed as she walked up to the window. Only to find it empty.

Duke wasn't there.

You waited too long. Someone else bought him.

The disappointment that came over her was perplexing. Why did she care so much about that dog?

Maybe they hadn't sold Duke. Maybe the store owner had taken him out for a walk. Katie pushed inside the pet store, hoping that was, indeed, the case.

"Hello," greeted the friendly faced woman behind the counter.

"Hi."

"You're the one who's always coming in here to play with the cocker spaniel, aren't you?"

Katie nodded. "I noticed he wasn't in the window."

The woman's eyes lit up. "Someone bought him, only an hour or so ago."

You're too late. That's what happens when you're afraid to commit.

A lump welled in Katie's throat and she had to blink hard to keep from crying. God, this was so stupid. Getting misty-eyed over a puppy who wasn't even hers. "Did he go to a good home?"

"A very good home." The pet-shop woman nodded. "The man said he was buying him as a surprise for his girlfriend. Apparently she's always wanted a dog, but circumstances have prevented her from owning one until now."

"It's good he's found a great home." Katie forced a smile. "I'm happy. So happy."

Quickly, she turned and hurried from the pet shop. She thought of the dog collar Liam had given her. She'd never get to use it on Duke.

She didn't feel like heading home, but she didn't want to go to a bar by herself. Not knowing what else to do, she headed for the park.

She walked down the path sniffling into a tissue, telling herself she was sad because Duke was no longer in the window. Denying that her sorrow had anything to do with Liam.

The air was cool but not unpleasantly so. Autumn leaves gusted across the sidewalk. On the yellowing grass, a group of teenage boys played football, laughing and tussling. She could hear the city traffic passing by and in the distance, the sound of a dog barking.

She skirted the pond, watching the ducks swim gracefully across the water and remembered the day Duke had pulled her in. She remembered Liam's apartment, and her heart swelled against the bittersweet memory. In three short weeks, she'd lost them both, Duke and Liam.

A trio of women on in-line skates scooted past her. The barking dog was getting closer. She passed a park bench where an elderly couple sat holding hands and watching the birds bedding down in the trees before nightfall.

She rounded a corner and up ahead she saw a man in a beige trench coat walking a dog.

It was a cocker spaniel who looked just like Duke.

The dog's barking grew more frantic as he pulled on his owner's leash.

Katie's eyes went from the dog to the man.

Liam!

She didn't know what to do, so she just stood there, waiting for him to get closer. But Duke wasn't into the games people play when they're falling in love. He jerked the leash from Liam's hand and came barreling straight toward her, his long curly ears flapping as he ran.

She dropped to her knees and scooped the cocker spaniel into her arms. He greeted her with a wriggling tail and exuberant tongue. Liam couldn't have given her a better gift if he'd presented her with the title to his Lamborghini. "The pet-shop lady told me some man had bought him for his girlfriend."

"He did," Liam said.

Katie's eyes met his. "You bought Duke for me?"

"I did."

"But my condo won't let me keep pets."

"You could always move."

"Where to?"

"I was hoping," his voice cracked, "you'd consider moving in with me. But if it's too soon for that, there's a vacant apartment in my building."

LIAM WATCHED HER set the puppy on the ground and stand up to face him. Her soft blond hair floated loosely about her shoulders in a sexy tumble. Her lips were painted a luscious shade of raspberry. She was dressed in black tailored slacks, a starched white blouse and tweed blazer. She looked sophisticated, relaxed and utterly beautiful.

"I can't answer that question the way you want me to answer."

He pulled in a breath. He was hoping giving her the dog would be enough to get back into her good graces. He should have known it wouldn't be that easy. "I screwed up, Katie. I know it. I can't tell you how sorry I am."

It hurt him to see her eyes were red-rimmed and she held a tissue clutched tight in her hand. She'd been crying, and he was terrified he was the cause of it. He reached to touch her forearm, but she shied away.

"You really pulled the rug out from under me, Liam. I was finally ready to take a chance on love and when I did, when I dared to lower my guard and make myself vulnerable, you walked out on me."

"I had a lot of time to think on the flight home and I

didn't like what I realized about myself. I was projecting my guilt about not admitting who I really was onto you. I went to see Finn Delancy and I confronted him."

"What happened?"

"He denied he was my father."

"So nothing was resolved?"

"No," he said. "I finally figured out there was nothing to resolve. I don't need Finn Delancy to validate me. I don't need the fortune I've amassed to prove I'm a worthy human being."

"So where does this leave us?"

"Right here." Liam couldn't stand not touching her again. He reached out, took her hands and slowly pulled her toward him.

"All the old resentment toward Delancy is gone?"

"Every bit of it. How about you?"

She nodded. "I feel great. No, better than great. I feel free."

"Me, too."

"What about your work? What's going to replace the drive in your life now that Delancy no longer matters to you?" she asked.

"I was hoping you could help me find a way to fill that void."

A small smile appeared on her lips. "I think maybe we could work something out."

"I want to make this work, Katie. I want it so badly. More than I've ever wanted anything, even getting back at my father."

"You've forgiven me for using you to complete my Martini dares?"

"I was never mad at you."

"No? Because it sure felt like it."

He shook his head. "I was afraid. Afraid of what I was feeling. Afraid that I could never be man enough for a woman like you."

She cupped his cheek with her palm and gazed at him with such tenderness it made his heart hurt.

"What changed your mind?"

"You did. Your strength and courage inspired me. You were brave enough to do those dares, to put yourself on the line. I had to try. I couldn't go through the rest of my life not knowing what might have been."

KATIE STARED into his hazel eyes at the vulnerable man behind the suave facade. What she saw reflected there moved her deeply and swept away any remaining doubts she harbored. Liam had no idea the value of his own worth, but she was determined to teach him.

"I'm ready to start fresh," he said. "If you'll forgive me. I've made a lot a mistakes and, I swear, I'll do my best to make up for them."

"It's already over. Forgiven and forgotten," she said.

"Katie." He kissed her there on the sidewalk while Duke ran in circles around their feet, tangling them up in his leash.

"No more secrets between us," Liam said, breaking the kiss to stare into her eyes. "Not even silly ones."

"No more secrets," she promised.

"I respect you, I admire you, I envy the courageous way you love so fully, so easily. You're my hero, Katie Winfield."

"Really?" Her heart filled with emotion.

He hitched in his breath. "And I love you, Katie, and I don't throw those words around lightly. In fact, other than my mother, you're the only one I've ever said them to."

She could tell how much it cost him to admit his feelings. He was used to tamping them down, hiding from tender emotions. But here he was laying himself bare, putting his heart on the line for her.

"Thank you, Liam," she said, "for that most treasured gift."

He'd said the words she'd most needed to hear. He made her feel cherished and prized and that her opinions were valued.

"You've saved me from myself." He touched his forehead against hers and stared deeply into her eyes.

"Oh, Liam." She wrapped her arms around his neck. "I love you, too."

THEY WENT BACK to Liam's place. They fed and watered Duke and made him a pallet on the floor.

Without another word, Liam took off his clothes and undressed her slowly, carefully, and then led her to his bed. When his fingers touched her bare skin, her nerve endings dissolved into a pool of liquid fire.

For Liam, this was all about her pleasure. Nothing mattered more to him than this glorious woman, who'd not only turned his world upside down but twisted his heart inside out and changed everything he knew.

All these years, he'd believed he would never really find where he belonged. He'd been so very wrong. He belonged right here with Katie.

The provocative little moan that escaped her as his fingers kneaded her bare backside caught him low in the gut and inflamed his passion, the way she always did.

Why on earth had he ever placed thoughts of revenge above acts of love? In less than a month of knowing her, she'd given him so much. He vowed to spend the rest of his life giving back more than he got. And if that included dressing up like a pirate, or making love in the balcony of a theatre, then by gosh, he'd willingly do it for her.

He leaned down to kiss the nape of her neck, but before he got there, she rolled over onto her back and looked up into his eyes with such love it took his breath away.

"Get over here," she said, wrapped her arms around his neck and pulled him toward her.

"Now we're talking." His body hardened with anticipation as he thought of all the fun that lay ahead of them. She tugged his head down to hers and kissed him with a deep, wet passionate kiss that told him he was the luckiest man in the world.

He settled his body over hers, bracing his weight on his forearms, and looked deeply into her eyes.

"I love you, Katie Winfield, now, tomorrow, always."

"Oh, Liam," she said. "That's all I ever wanted to hear."

He enveloped her in his arms, listened to the pounding of her heart. He felt truly immortal.

Then they nibbled and licked and touched and suckled. They took their time, fully getting to know each other. No surprises, no disguises.

Just true and honest loving.

The hours streamed by in a blur of sensuous heat, the sating of sexual longings, until at the very stroke of midnight, their two souls merged as one. They knew there would never be any more secrets between them.

Love had changed the physics of their lives and re-drawn the boundary of what they'd believed about the world and the magic that was truly possible.

And as they reached love's glorious pinnacle, separated only by the thinnest rind of skin, their fate was sealed, their destinies forever intertwined.

15

WHEN HER CELL PHONE rang the next morning, Katie rolled over with a smile on her face. She glanced to see Liam asleep beside her and Duke dozing at the foot of the bed. Her grin widened. It wasn't a dream. Quietly, she slipped out of the bed and snatched her purse up off the floor, digging out her cell phone on the fly as she hustled to the living room.

"Hello."

"Katie, where are you? I went by your condo to see if you wanted to do breakfast but you weren't there."

"Brooke, how are you?" She felt so wonderful she wanted to share her joy with her sister but wasn't sure how she would feel about the news that Katie and Liam were an item.

"I think I'm finally feeling strong enough to go through mother's things. Joey's up for it, too. How about you?"

Sorting through their mother's personal effects was going to be an emotional experience and until now, she'd rigorously avoided it. Honestly, all three of them had. But it needed to be done. And being with Liam had given Katie the courage she needed to face her shortcomings and problems in the moment, and deal with them.

"When?"

"You'll come?"

"Yes."

"This afternoon."

"I'll be there."

"You sound different," Brooke observed.

"How so?"

"You sound like you've accepted Mom's death."

Katie realized it was true. At some point, she'd let go of her anger. She'd learned to handle her fears honestly and to stop hiding from herself. And in the process, she'd learned to accept the world as it was.

Even though she was sad her mother was gone, she had her memories. So many great memories.

"Actually," Katie said, "I'm looking forward to doing this. It's time to give up the grieving and celebrate Mom's life."

Brooke made a tiny noise of surprise. "You sound so mature and responsible."

That acknowledgement from her sister tightened Katie's throat with emotion. "A lot's happened to me lately. I'll tell you about it when I get there."

Several hours later, after she and Liam had bonded over breakfast in bed, Katie arrived at her family's home. Her sisters were already there, sitting cross-legged on the floor of their mother's bedroom looking at photo albums, a box of tissues sitting between them.

"Katie," Brooke said, getting to her feet to hug her.

How incredibly beautiful her sister was with her dreamy light brown eyes, long, silky caramel-colored hair and arched widow's peak. They didn't know where Brooke had inherited it. No one else in the family had one.

Her oldest sister possessed a seriousness that Katie lacked. But Brooke also had a way about her that instantly put others at ease. She was soothing as warm milk on a cold winter night. She wore simple, tailored clothes in muted, don't-notice-me colors, which was odd for an artistic woman who dressed windows for the most exclusive department store in Boston.

Brooke pulled back and gave Katie the once over. "You're glowing. You look…*happy.*"

"You look like a woman in love," Joey commented.

She was aware of the heat of her sister's gaze on her face. Joey was a lawyer and quite perceptive. Taller than Katie, she was also thinner, with the lithe gait of a dancer. Her hair was styled in a sleek cut that softened her angular face. She had a Mensa IQ and a wickedly sharp sense of humor that often belied her good-girl image.

At her sisters' comments, Katie could contain herself no longer. A broad smile broke across her face. "I am in love!"

"That's wonderful," Joey said, and hugged Katie, too.

Brooke splayed a hand over her heart. "Who is he?"

Here was the hard part. Katie faced Brooke. "I hope you're not going to be to upset with me, but it's Liam James."

"Well, I am a bit surprised, but why would I be mad? Liam and I are just friends and he's a wonderful guy. I'm so happy you two found each other."

"It's been incredible." Katie had to blink to keep tears of joy from welling up in her eyes.

Joey scooped their mother's keepsake box up off the floor. "This calls for a celebration. I'll put on some tea. Brooke can break out that tin of cookies from Worthington's. And you can tell us how you hooked up with *Young Bostonian*'s most eligible bachelor, while we go through the keepsake box."

"Mom would approve." Brooke nodded.

Katie followed her sisters through the house to the large kitchen where their mother had spent most of her time. Even though they'd had maids, unlike many Beacon Hill Brahmins, Daisy Winfield had preferred to make meals for her family rather than turn the chore over to a professional cook.

Joey put the kettle on and Brooke got out the cookies. Katie took a seat at the kitchen table and opened up the keepsake box. A few minutes later her sisters joined her at the table, armed with cups of Earl Grey and a platter of Scottish shortbread.

They listened while Katie told them about the Ladies League Ball and what had happened in the closet. When she got to the part about getting a letter from Lindsay Beckham about her Martinis and Bikinis group, Joey put down her cup of tea.

"I got one of those," Joey said. "I tossed it away."

"I got one, as well," Brooke admitted. "I hung on to mine. I thought I might go next month."

"You can come with me," Katie invited. "Because I gotta tell you, this dare stuff works. Although I have to admit there were times when I thought everything was coming unraveled."

"What do you mean?"

Katie finished telling them all that had transpired with her three dares. From her tryst with Liam in the movie theatre, to their trip to Fiji, to the miscommunication that had almost torn them apart.

"Wow," Brooke said when she'd finished. "Maybe I will give this Martinis and Bikinis group a shot."

"It certainly sounds like you found your match with Liam," Joey said. It might have been her imagination, but Katie could have sworn her older sister sounded a wee bit envious of her newfound happiness.

Katie took a deep breath. "The Martini dares have certainly empowered me. If I hadn't gone through all that, I don't think I could be with you here today, going through Mom's things."

At that, the three women turned their attention to the box in front of Katie.

"We might as well dive in," Brooke said.

Katie took a deep breath and removed the lid from the box. On top were the Valentine's Day cards they'd made for their mother when they were children. Red construction paper, crayon lettering, paper lace. Katie took them out and passed them around to her sisters. They looked at the cards one by one, reading I LOVE YOU MOMMY written in messy, childish print.

Underneath the cards, Katie found locks of their hair from their first haircuts, graphed growth charts and their baby booties. There were report cards, school pictures and good-conduct medals for Joey and Brooke. And there was a faded Polaroid of Katie holding the first Duke with a happy, gap-toothed grin on her face.

Tears slipped down their faces at the childhood treasures their mother had saved. Brooke passed out tissues. They laughed and cried and talked and remembered their mother's life. They drank tea and scarfed cookies and bonded in a way they hadn't in a long time.

Then hours later, as they neared the bottom of the big wooden keepsake box, they discovered something curious.

It was a large yellow envelope that was sealed. On the outside, in Daisy's handwriting, they read, *To be opened by my daughters, Brooke, Joey and Katie, on the event of my death.*

A sudden chill of dread ran down Katie's spine.

"What's this?" Brooke frowned and reached for the envelope.

"Go ahead and open it," Joey said. "You're the oldest."

Brooke broke the seal and dumped the contents out on the table.

A second envelope and baby pictures. But not of Brooke or Joey or Katie. They flipped through the pictures, watching the little girl grow from a serious-faced baby to a serious-faced young girl.

"Who's this?" Brooke asked.

"Maybe it's one of Mom's relatives that she never talked about."

"Flip the photos over and see if there's a name on the back," Joey suggested.

Brooked turned over the picture she had in her hand.

In one snapshot, the girl was about four, staring churlishly at the camera.

"Lindsay, age four years, three months," Brooke read aloud.

"Hey," Joey said, as she opened the second envelope, "these are legal papers."

The raised hairs on the nape of her neck made Katie afraid to ask, but she was compelled. The little girl looked strangely familiar and the name Lindsay struck a certain resonance inside her. "What kind of legal papers?"

Joey raised her head from the paperwork to meet her sisters' gazes. "Adoption papers."

"Mom and Dad adopted a kid we knew nothing about? What happened to her?"

Joey's face paled as she read on. "No, Mom had a child no one knew anything about. A child she gave up for adoption before she met Dad and now she wants us to find her."

"Who is she?"

"Her name," Joey said, "is Lindsay Beckham."

* * * * *

Don't miss Brooke's story and the continuation of the Martini Dares miniseries,
MY FRONT PAGE SCANDAL
by Carrie Alexander,
coming next month from Harlequin Blaze!

For a sneak preview of Marie Ferrarella's
DOCTOR IN THE HOUSE,
coming to NEXT in September,
please turn the page.

He didn't look like an unholy terror.

But maybe that reputation was exaggerated, Bailey DelMonico thought as she turned in her chair to look toward the doorway.

The man didn't seem scary at all.

Dr. Munro, or Ivan the Terrible, was tall, with an athletic build and wide shoulders. The cheekbones beneath what she estimated to be day-old stubble were prominent. His hair was light brown and just this side of unruly. Munro's hair looked as if he used his fingers for a comb and didn't care who knew it.

The eyes were brown, almost black as they were aimed at her. There was no other word for it. Aimed. As if he was debating whether or not to fire at point-blank range.

Somewhere in the back of her mind, a line from a B movie, "Be afraid—be very afraid..." whispered along the perimeter of her brain. Warning her. Almost against her will, it caused her to brace her shoulders. Bailey had to remind herself to breathe in and out like a normal person.

The chief of staff, Dr. Bennett, had tried his level best to put her at ease and had almost succeeded. But an air of tension had entered with Munro. She wondered if Dr.

Bennett was bracing himself, as well, bracing for some kind of disaster or explosion.

"Ah, here he is now," Harold Bennett announced needlessly. The smile on his lips was slightly forced, and the look in his gray, kindly eyes held a warning as he looked at his chief neurosurgeon. "We were just talking about you, Dr. Munro."

"Can't imagine why," Ivan replied dryly.

Harold cleared his throat, as if that would cover the less than friendly tone of voice Ivan had just displayed. "Dr. Munro, this is the young woman I was telling you about yesterday."

Now his eyes dissected her. Bailey felt as if she was undergoing a scalpel-less autopsy right then and there. "Ah, yes, the Stanford Special."

He made her sound like something that was listed at the top of a third-rate diner menu. There was enough contempt in his voice to offend an entire delegation from the UN.

Summoning the bravado that her parents always claimed had been infused in her since the moment she first drew breath, Bailey put out her hand. "Hello. I'm Dr. Bailey DelMonico."

Ivan made no effort to take the hand offered to him. Instead, he slid his long, lanky form bonelessly into the chair beside her. He proceeded to move the chair ever so slightly so that there was even more space between them. Ivan faced the chief of staff, but the words he spoke were addressed to her.

"You're a doctor, DelMonico, when I say you're a doctor," he informed her coldly, sparing her only one frosty glance to punctuate the end of his statement.

Harold stifled a sigh. "Dr. Munro is going to take over your education. Dr. Munro—" he fixed Ivan with a steely gaze that had been known to send lesser doctors running for their antacids, but, as always, seemed to have no effect on the chief neurosurgeon "—I want you to award her every consideration. From now on, Dr. DelMonico is to be your shadow, your sponge and your assistant." He emphasized the last word as his eyes locked with Ivan's. "Do I make myself clear?"

For his part, Ivan seemed completely unfazed. He merely nodded, his eyes and expression unreadable. "Perfectly."

His hand was on the doorknob. Bailey sprang to her feet. Her chair made a scraping noise as she moved it back and then quickly joined the neurosurgeon before he could leave the office.

Closing the door behind him, Ivan leaned over and whispered into her ear, "Just so you know, I'm going to be your worst nightmare."

Bailey DelMonico has finally
gotten her life on track, and is
passionate about her recent career
change. Nothing will stand in the way
of her becoming a doctor...that is,
until she's paired with the sharp-tongued
Dr. Ivan Munro.

Watch the sparks fly in

Doctor in the House

by *USA TODAY* Bestselling Author
Marie Ferrarella

Available September 2007

Intrigued? Read more at
TheNextNovel.com

HARLEQUIN®
Next™

HN88141

nocturne™

Look for

NIGHT MISCHIEF

by

NINA BRUHNS

Lady Dawn Maybank's worst nightmare
is realized when she accidentally conjures
a demon of vengeance, Galen McManus. What
she doesn't realize is that Galen plans to teach
her a lesson in love—one she'll never forget....

DARK
ENCHANTMENTS

Available October wherever you buy books.

*Don't miss the last installment of Dark Enchantments,
SAVING DESTINY by Pat White, available November.*

REQUEST YOUR FREE BOOKS!

2 FREE NOVELS PLUS 2 FREE GIFTS!

HARLEQUIN®

Blaze®

Red-hot reads!

YES! Please send me 2 FREE Harlequin® Blaze® novels and my 2 FREE gifts. After receiving them, if I don't wish to receive any more books, I can return the shipping statement marked "cancel." If I don't cancel, I will receive 6 brand-new novels every month and be billed just $3.99 per book in the U.S., or $4.47 per book in Canada, plus 25¢ shipping and handling per book and applicable taxes, if any*. That's a savings of at least 15% off the cover price! I understand that accepting the 2 free books and gifts places me under no obligation to buy anything. I can always return a shipment and cancel at any time. Even if I never buy another book from Harlequin, the two free books and gifts are mine to keep forever.

151 HDN EF3W   351 HDN EF3X

Name	(PLEASE PRINT)	
Address		Apt.
City	State/Prov.	Zip/Postal Code

Signature (if under 18, a parent or guardian must sign)

Mail to the **Harlequin Reader Service**®:
IN U.S.A.: P.O. Box 1867, Buffalo, NY 14240-1867
IN CANADA: P.O. Box 609, Fort Erie, Ontario L2A 5X3

Not valid to current Harlequin Blaze subscribers.

Want to try two free books from another line?
Call 1-800-873-8635 or visit www.morefreebooks.com.

* Terms and prices subject to change without notice. NY residents add applicable sales tax. Canadian residents will be charged applicable provincial taxes and GST. This offer is limited to one order per household. All orders subject to approval. Credit or debit balances in a customer's account(s) may be offset by any other outstanding balance owed by or to the customer. Please allow 4 to 6 weeks for delivery.

Your Privacy: Harlequin is committed to protecting your privacy. Our Privacy Policy is available online at www.eHarlequin.com or upon request from the Reader Service. From time to time we make our lists of customers available to reputable firms who may have a product or service of interest to you. If you would prefer we not share your name and address, please check here. ☐

HB07

HARLEQUIN Romance

New York Times bestselling author

DIANA PALMER

Handsome, eligible ranch owner Stuart York knew
Ivy Conley was too young for him, so he closed his heart
to her and sent her away—despite the fireworks between
them. Now, years later, Ivy is determined not to be
treated like a little girl anymore...but for some reason,
Stuart is always fighting her battles for her. And safe in
Stuart's arms makes Ivy feel like a woman...his woman.

Winter Roses

Available November.

HRIBC03985

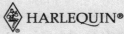

COMING NEXT MONTH

#351 IF HE ONLY KNEW... Debbi Rawlins
Men To Do

At Sara Wells's impromptu farewell party, coworker Cody Shea gives her a sizzling and unexpected kiss. Now, he may think this is the end, but given the hidden fantasies Sara's always had about the hot Manhattan litigator, this could be the beginning of a long goodbye....

#352 MY FRONT PAGE SCANDAL Carrie Alexander
The Martini Dares, Bk. 2

Bad boy David Carrera is the catalyst Brooke Winfield needs to release her inner wild child. His daring makes her throw off her conservative upbringing...not to mention her clothes. But will she still feel that way when their sexy exploits become front-page news?

#353 FLYBOY Karen Foley

A secret corporate club that promotes men who get down and dirty on business travel? Once aerospace engineer Sedona Stewart finds out why she isn't being promoted, she's ready to quit. But then she's assigned to work with sexy fighter pilot Angel Torres. And suddenly she's tempted to get a little down and dirty herself....

#354 SHOCK WAVES Colleen Collins
Sex on the Beach, Bk. 2

A makeover isn't exactly what Ellie Rockwell planned for her beach vacation. But losing her goth-girl look lands her a spot on her favorite TV show...and the eye of her teenage crush Bill Romero. Now that they're both adults, there's no end to the fun they can have.

#355 COLD CASE, HOT BODIES Jule McBride
The Wrong Bed

Start with a drop-dead-gorgeous cop and a heroine linked to an old murder case. Add a haunted town house in the Five Points area of New York City, and it equals a supremely sexy game of cat and mouse for Dario Donato and Cassidy Case. But their staying one step ahead of the killer seems less dangerous than the scorching heat between them!

#356 FOR LUST OR MONEY Kate Hoffmann
Million Dollar Secrets, Bk. 4

One minute thirty-five-year-old actress Kelly Castelle is pretty well washed-up. The next she's in a new city with all kinds of prospects—and an incredibly hot guy in her bed. Zach Haas is sexy, adventurous...and twenty-four years old. The affair is everything she's ever dreamed about. Only, dreams aren't meant to last....

www.eHarlequin.com

HBCNM0907